entra
hin Ce

Dedalus Euro Shorts
General Editor: Mike Mitchell

Las Adventures
des
Inspector Cabillot

Diego Marani

Las Adventures des Inspector Cabillot

Dedalus

Published in the UK by Dedalus Limited,
24-26, St Judith's Lane, Sawtry, Cambs, PE28 5XE
email: info@dedalusbooks.com
www.dedalusbooks.com

ISBN 978 1 907650 59 8

Dedalus is distributed in the USA and Canada by SCB Distributors,
15608 South New Century Drive, Gardena, CA 90248
email: info@scbdistributors.com   web: www.scbdistributors.com

Dedalus is distributed in Australia by Peribo Pty Ltd.
58, Beaumont Road, Mount Kuring-gai, N.S.W. 2080
email: info@peribo.com.au

First published by Dedalus in 2012
Las Adventures des Inspector Cabillot copyright © Diego Marani 2012
Published by arrangement with Marco Vigevani Agenzia Letteraria

Printed in Finland by Bookwell
Typeset by Marie Lane

A C.I.P. listing for this book is available on request.

Der Authore

Diego Marani esse eine Italianse writer und Europeane Union officer. In Brussels livingante, el invented der wunderfulle und mucho irreverente lingua des Europanto, eine mix van differente linguas sonder grammatica und regulationes. Europanto esse der jazz des linguas. Keine study necessite, just improviste, und tu shal siempre fluente esse in diese most amusingante lingua.

Diego Marani habe gewritten manige articulos in Europanto in multiple Europeane journalos, tambien eine videoclip, canzones und some theatre pieces. Diego Marani esse toch best renamed por seine Italianse novellas und collabore in Italianse lingua mit some culturale Italianse journalos.

Introductione

Twalwe jahros after seine first publicatione, *Las Adventures des Inspector Cabillot* disbarke in Grosse Britannie unter populare request. Inspector Cabillot, der primero Europeane detective, disfronte manige Europeane topicos, als eine madde bovine terroriste cellula dat agresse London und der kidnappingo van eine prestigiose Europeane leader by eine Finnische nationaliste gruppe die want Europanto mit Finnische replace als unique lingua des Europeane Unione. Alles stories inspire eine joyfulle visione des Europeane Unione und seine problemas in eine playfulle lingua invented por make Europeanos tenfinally reciproque understande, or desminder grandemente laughe.

Inspector Cabillot esse der autentiquo europeane polizero, fightingante contra der evil por eine Europa van pax und prosperity donde man speake eine unique lingua: Europanto.

1

Cabillot und der mysterio
des exotische pralinas

Was eine frigid morning van Octubre in Brussel. Die arbor des park was rubiconde, die benches floatingantes in eine caliginose fog. Sommige laborantes maghrebinos was der garbage collectingante terwhile singing melancholique tunes. Op der 50th floor des Europeane Polizei Tower der Chef Inspector General des Service des Bizarre Affairs, Capitain What, frapped op der tabula und dixit:"Dat esse keine joke! Call rapido Cabillot!".

Inspector Cabillot put seine Europanto crossverba under der desk, hanged der telefono und jumped op der cuirassed liftor por emergence cases.

"Moi demanded, Captain What?"

"Ja. Ich habe eine delicate mission por you. Als you know, die europeanos countries send plenty aid zum developingantes countries und superalles, butter, second hand bicyclos, italian beer, english vino, germanische fashion, olde stamps, greek horloges, rumenian shoes und bulgarische used tyres. Well, some van diese aid never arrive zum destinatione. There must esse eine hole someplatz in Sudamerica, plus exacto in der Petite Guyane Luxembourgeoise. There esse tambien eine klinika por invalidos europeanos polizeros die esse eine poquito suspecta. Ich want dat you make eine enquest, inspector. You shal pretende de esse eine invalido Europeano polizero und make toiself hospitalized. Sergent Otto Oliveira van der Europeane Polizei Brigade por Paranormale Eventos (EPOBRIFOPAREV) shal mit you in touch permane und toi assiste from Brussel.

"Yesful, Captain What! Zum teine orders!"

"Remember dat esse superalles der butter que disvanish und wir habe keine indices. Gutte fortune, inspector!"

Inspector Cabillot got back in seine oficina zum prepare baggages.

"What bring man in der Petite Guyane Luxembourgeoise, Otto?" asked aan seine beste collaborator.

"Ich know nicht... maybe eine fishing cane, eine warmewater bouteilla, somechose zum lecture oder eine pleasingante muchacha. Aber dat can tambien op place finden..."

Inspector Cabillot put in der baggage case der Lisbon Treaty, some Europanto crossverba, seine flowered bermudas, eine straw casque und eine vocabulario Guyanish-Europanto.

Der followingante dag, Inspector Cabillot gelanded at Paramarange, der capitalcity des Petite Guyane Luxembourgeoise mit der same avioplano der Europeano aid transportante. Paramarange esse eine maritime tropicale city mit mucho people und eine grosse harbour. Subito Cabillot remarqued dat almost alles paramarangos were plumpos obesos als porcadillos. Alleswhere was full van chocolate reklames und alles boutiques was full van alles sortes pralinas.

"Man must aquì chocolate like muchissimo" esclamed Cabillot aan der taximanno.

"Certainly Segnor! Wir produce aquì die beste chocolates des mundo! People come out van Switzerlandia por unsere chocolates kauffe. Where esse you addressingante?"

"Aan der klinika 'Hemelpax' "

Diego Marani

"Oh, esse you eine van diese very mucho nervouse people?"
"Mucho, muchissimo nervouse..." repliqued der inspector, und der taximanno suddenlemente silenced.

Der klinika was eine moderne buildingo, mit blanco muros, verde fenestras und florido garden. Aan der entranza was Dr. Guzman, der director des klinika, expectante.
"Herr Cabillot, Ich suppose..."
"In persona, Herr Doctor!"
"Bienkomen in Hemelpax! Alsyoubitte, sich make comfortable in meine officio! Frau Hassenpain, prepare please de stanza 23!"
Dr. Guzman reclosed der porta und sitted in seine poltronchair.
"Illustrissime Cabillot, you shal remarque dat aquì man stay in pax und rest. Der nightcauchemare des Europa wil presto become eine distante memoria por you tambien. Ich know dat you esse keine grave case, aber toch man must prudente esse mit mentale maladias. Eine mucho importante recommandation: remember de never pronounce aquì der parola Europa. Habe aquì people die quando this parola entende, jump op air als furiosos psychique enflammados und start zum sobbe, disperantes, mucho clamor makeantes, die hairs sich arrachantes van der kopf, alles tremblingantes als diabolische possessed. Aquì man superalles must sleep, placide sleep und alles forgette. Thinque aan nada, empty der kopf. In der postmeridio esse sommige activitates distractivas, als der promenada in der park oder eine fussballe match. Op der suntag postmeridio esse der projection des film, siempre der same one, por not trouble die fragiles esprits des malades: "Bambi". Ich maxime hope que you shal aquì happy esse.

You can ahora eine promenade habe around des city. Aquì man manduca at sept ,o cloque. Basta der vista, Herr Cabillot! Acquainte mit teine nova home!"

Der doctor stande op und accompanied Cabillot aan der porta. Cabillot sortante, remarqued Frau Hassenpain out des fenestra spyante.

Paramarange ist eine very bombardose city und der pueblo esse calorosissimo. Everytodo manducate pralinas non-stop und when manducate tropo mucho, man beginne dance der Tarabomba, eine tipique paramarangse rythmo, very desfrenado und perambulante. Dat eveningo, in die stradas was plenty van "tarabombos" (die danceros de Tarabomba) exaltados dancingantes under der heat des settingante sonne. In eine café op der plaza, Cabillot tasted sommige pralinas und ello tambien was captured by der urgente lust de dance de Tarabomba. Der inspector joined de dance und muchachas prosperosas enveloped seine kopf mit multicolore flowers. Op dinner, in der restorante des klinika, Cabillot manducated authentiquas paramarangas specialitades:

Moules au chocolat
Emincé de mouette au cacao avec pralines frites
Salade aux quatre chocolats
Chocolat chaud (cuvée 1978)

"Eine poquito butter?" pregunted Frau Hassenpain der dish servingante.

"Nein, bedankes, Ich liebe butter nicht. Ich esse allergique aan butter" responded Cabillot.

Aber Frau Hassenpain let der butter over des tabula. 'Strange Frau', thinked Cabillot. Around ello, andere pazientos des klinika was silentes manducantes, mit eyos grande open, blancos als in der ice gefrozen essed. Diese nacht Cabillot sleeped uncomfortable und dreamed grosse waitresses mestizas de Tarabomba on der la playa in topless dancingantes. Promiscuose smilingantes, ellas approched der inspector, die tittones shakerantes mit mucho flaccido und humido chap, chap.

Der morgen, Cabillot went explorante eine poquito in der klinika. Sometimes ello hadde der impression eine extrange sound auscultate, like motores turningantes. Ello climbed op und descended alles floors, dat strange noise persistente. Impossible de track seine provenience. Cabillot attempted der underground cave descende. Aber der porta was closed mit grosse lock. Der inspector mumbled und eine suspecto seine kopf inflammed.

Por der breakfasto, preferred de manducate juste eine tea cuppe mit biscuitos. Ello hadde eine laboriosa digestion und wanted seine stomach preserve van acid surprisas.

"Sommige butter?" proposed again insistente Frau Hassenpain.

"Already dixit dat Ich manducate butter nicht, bedankes. Ich esse allergique aan butter" responded mit eine kleine irritatione Cabillot.

Durante alles dag, Cabillot permanente op der terrasse des klinika, die mosquitos smashingantes und der paramarango journalo "El Postmeridio" lecturingante. Andere pazientes was op der terrasse sunbronzante. Ellos was solitaire speakingantes, oder mit dolly bambolas playingantes. Discrete infirmeros was stricte surveillantes. Cabillot hadde der feeling dat sommige anormale was happeningante in diese extrange platz, aber could nicht unterstande wat. Diese nacht tambien der inspector coudde slapen nicht. Es was again diese mysteriose noise, from die profunde partes des buildingo repercussante. Op mucho tardive nacht, Cabillot decided de go again explorante. Descendendo in der hall, suddenlemente ausculted eine scream van terror. Der inspector went runningante nach der kitchen. Op der floor stabat Frau Hassenpain, mit eine knife enfonced in der belly und der mouth full van chocolate.

Der kommissar des paramarangse polizei, Herr Lesferre, fixed Cabillot in die eyos und dixit:

"Suicidio. Esse klaro! Frau Hassenpain was eine chocolate robberesse. Diese nacht improvistamente sich repented und because des shame de esse eine criminal, decided de sichself slaughterate mit der knife! Eine terrible einde... Wat thinke, inspector?"

Inspector Cabillot op diese momento thinked aan todo der evil dat can provoque exessive Derrick op TV. Nodded silenciose und exit des kitchen.

Later diese morningo, in der restorante, Cabillot was seine matinale chocolate drinkingante quando remarqued eine paquet van butter op seine tabula. Regarded distractemente und permaned reflexive. Die tabulas was siempre prepared by Frau Hassenpain op der eveningo, after des dinner. Suddenlemente, der Inspector unterstudde. Dann subito jumped from seine platz. Got nach der telefono und appelled der operator.

"Mit de Europeane Polizei in Brussel, alsyoubitte!"

Sudden eine clamoroso shout blasted in der restorante: alles die pazientes were die hair self arrachantes, super die tabulas jumpantes mit die eyos out des kopf. Eine equipo van infirmeros came mit grosse syringues van eine black liquido full.

"Wat esse diese liquido?" pregunted Cabillot aan Dr. Guzman subito rushingante in de stanza.

"Chocolate calmante. Inspector, Ich recommanded you de never pronounce die parola Europa aquì!"

"Mucho desolated, Doctor... Ich was distracted."

Cabillot returned aan der telefono.

"Hallococco ? Ja, passe moi Otto Oliveira, alsyoubitte! Otto? Cabillot speakeante. Listen moi carefullemente. Habe you der lista des aids des Europa aan der Petite Guyane Luxembourgeoise? Gut, lecture moi please!"

"Yesful Inspector! Hondred bottles detergent antikalk por W.C., hondred box Monopoly game, thousandoquinquo-hondredzwei tennis raquettes, quinquanta roller-skates, zwei box biscuitos, thousandzvingtres autoradios, quatro tons multicolor plasticine, quinquanta litros Orangina drink, sep-thondredquarantafive box hair teintura blonde, eine kilo ba-nanas, huithondredtrentaseven box raviolis, eine hondredsex-antanine paquets intieme pampers..."

"Gut, gut! Dat esse bastante. Now lecture lista aid por die victimas des storm in Nordeuropa..."

"Yesful! Quatrehondredhuitantathree wind-surf, vingtfive hair-dryer, eine tank Chanel n°13, eine boxe Mekkano, zweihondertquatro box Viagra, troishondred containeros butter...

"Stop! Ach! Ja! Ich guessed correct! Dann you must moi helpen. You must exchange die troishonderd containeros butter mit troishonderd containeros vaseline! Unterstuddo?"

"Vaseline? Aan victimas des storm? Aber..."

"Discute nicht, Otto! Esse eine order! Basta der vista! Zum proximo!"

Cabillot exit des telefono box smilingante very much. Dr. Guzman regarded mumblingante. Eine worryngante shade obscured seine face.

"Doctor, eine question bitte" pregunted Cabillot, now mucho audaciose, "quantos many pazientes get aquì totalmente cured und recover mentale normalitate?"

"Desolated Inspector, nomanno aquì recover totalemente! Als you know, der life in de Europeane Polizei esse hard zum tolerate. Nerves explode, brain discompose. Man can aquì improve aber never completamente restore zum health. Die pazientes mit better resultos, only after ten jahros can again comics lecture und Zorro op TV watch without troubles. Scarcissime pazientes manage tambien de speak again. Aber ellos can pronounce only simplissime parolas, als "mama" oder "caca" oder "chocolate". Sfortunosamente, eine mucho rare course des maladia! Aber you esse keine terminale case, inspector. You can still eine almost normale life habe."

Inspector Cabillot ausculted cautiosemente. Now was der moment des action. Exit in de strada walkingante und calme expected seine trap zum release.

Diese nacht Cabillot hide sichself next des strada des avioporto. After zwei horas, improvisto eine column van camiones appeared out des dark und transited nach der klinika. In der shadow, Cabillot remarked plurimos hombres die camiones very presto und silentemente dischargeantes in der klinika storehaus. Der inspector was behind eine muro spyante quando eine stroke hit seine kopf. Cabillot fainted op soil ohne conscienze. Quando rewaked, was in eine blanca stanza, mit artifiziale neonica lux. Ello was gewrapped mit eine rope contra eine bed. Eine syringue was gestucked in seine arm. From eine kleine tube, eine liquido black flowed slowemente in seine veins. Dr. Guzman was watchingante mit maleficiose eyos. Laughingante dixit:

"Eh, eh, respectado Inspector! You shoudde nicht stick der nose in andere people business! Now you shal presto chocoaddicted become! Dat tube injecte kokoine in teine body, eine potente drogua! Tu shal eine perfecte chocojunky esse!"

"Dann Ich correcte supposed!" repliqued Cabillot, "kokoine esse toch in toda de paramarangse chocolate addizioned. Dat esse why everymundo dance de Tarabomba non stop und cannot refrain from bombastose behaviour! Todos esse exaltados toxicomanos! You esse eine bandido, Guzman! You robbe de butter des Europeano aid por Nordeuropa und dann produce aquì die drogua pralinas, in chocolate disguise! Ich esse sure dat teine laboratorio esse in diese unterground caves."

"Yesful indeed, inspector! Gut guessed! Aber tropo late! You shal nomanno diese historia raconte. You shal slave become van kokoine und shal slowemente mad furioso esse! Eine allucinated phantom! Ah, ah, ah!"

"Now unterstande... So als die invalidos polizeros. Esse keine invalidos aber toxicomanos!" accused der inspector. Und Guzman, poisonose admitted:

"Bravo Cabillot! Ellos esse, por so to say, amigos van moi! Ellos necessite meine droga por survive! Als ellos, you tambien shal become meine slave und shal obey meine orders!

Ich esse der plus powerfulle, Ich esse eine genius des evil! Ich shal der mundo presto dominate! Ah, ah, ah! Basta mit diese stupida klinika! Ich shal der primero, de unique chocodictator des mundo become! De Petite Guyane Luxembourgeoise shal become eine chocorepublic des cacao!"

Op diese momento, eine infirmero entered pantingante, mucho worried und troublissime speakante.

"Doctor, der pueblo esse op revolte! De ultime produkzion van pralinas esse abnormale! Unsere tecnicos unterstande nicht wat happened. Taste youself, bitte!"

Dr. Guzman, suspectoso eine pralinas in der mouth glissed.

"Puah! Wat esse diese merdenshit!"

"Vaseline, Herr Doctor! Gut por der skin!" interrupted Cabillot mit eine triumphante smile.

"Damnate sabotador! Ich shall toi kille mit meine hands!" exploded rageful Dr. Guzman, approachante der inspector mit rabidose gestures. Aber der infirmero alerted:

"Doctor, die toxicomanos furiosos habe de klinika invaded! Ellos seem mucho ferocitantes! Better escape quickemente!" cried der infirmero ful van terror. Dann der doctor unwillingante abandoned seine intentione de strangulate Cabillot. Mit der infirmero exit rocambolante out van eine secret porta. Rapido, eine wave de tarabombos ferocitantes desmashed der porta des klinika und assaulted die chocoine tubes, alles die beds renversantes por rage.

Inspector Cabillot managed de sich liberate. Eine poquito stoned, escaped from dat infernale platz.

In die avenidas und die plazas, der people was dementiale phagocytante mit incontrollate agitatione. Todos cried imprecantes, pantingantes, tarantellantes, die vestimentos stripoffantes, seine handen bitingantes und savagemente each andere smashante por conquest eine dose chocolate.

Alles die europeanos escaped des hotellos und refuge gefunde in der Nord Korea embassy por asyle politico pregunte. Actually, Nord Korea was der only country dat hadde diplomatische relaciones mit de Petite Guyane Luxembourgoeoise. Die journalistos was der koreane ambassador intervistantes, quando Cabillot arrived.

"Exellence, wat thinke about der unity des zwei Koreas?" was eine reporter preguntante.

"Zwei Koreas? Wat zwei?, Welke esse der secunda?" repliqued der ambassador seine cravate adjustante. Cabillot interrupted brutale der intervista und sich introduced:

"Inspector Cabillot van der Europese Polizei. Exellence, esse in Paramarange eine revoluzion. Eine criminalo, Dr. Guzman, intoxicated alles people mit kokoine, eine disruptive drug! Alles foreigneros residentes esse in dangero!"

"Keine worry, inspector! Meine ambassade got grosse muros. Quando young estudiante, Ich habe muros building in DDR estudied! Quick shal eine avioplano arrive und todos wil safe nach Europa travel."

"Exellence, noch eine problemito. Ich necessite presto ein poquito chokolade, bitte! Ich thinque dat Ich tambien habe eine abstinentia crisis! Helpe!"

"Oh, ja! Wir habe eine mucho savourite koreane soja chokolade. Shal dat suffice, inspector?" Cabillot fainted zum soil tremblingante.

Quando rewaked, ello was in der Europeane Polizei infirmaria van Brussel. Otto Oliveira was next seine bed.

"Inspector, how esse feelingante?" inquired solicitose und affectuose Otto.

"Mucho slecht! Wat happened in Paramarange?"

"Es was eine revoluzion und now eine chococommunist regime in der grasp des doctor Guzman mit der allianz des

Nord Korea."

"Ach! Dat was Ich mucho fearingante! Wat sfortunose development!"

"Aber raconte bitte, inspector. Wat toi happened! Tu disembarqued des avioplano in eine ambulanze, totale unconscious!" pregunted curioso Otto. Cabillot sitted op der bord des bed und raconted:

"Ich hadde todo unterstuddo when Ich remembered dat poor Frau Hassenpain, die secretaria des doctor, wanted meine attention attracte over der butter. Jedere morningo die dama proposed moi butter, quando claro was knowingante Ich liebe butter nicht. Ich explained dat Ich esse allergique. Manige times already dixit. Aber sfortunosemente, quando Ich alles unterstudde, es was trop late por Frau Hassenpain! Eine nacht founde her massacred op der kitchen floor."

"Inspector, er esse eine message por you," interrupted eine infirmero presto in der stanza enteringante.

"Eine message?"

Cabillot opened de enveloppa. Eine sentence was gewritten op eine chocolate papier: "No finish aquì! Wir shal encounter again por der finale combat! Dr. Guzman."

"Damnate criminal! Presto oder later Ich shal capture diese animal! Otto, bitte, give moi eine chokolate candy!"

"Desolated inspector! Der doctor dixit no chocolate. You must desintoxique! Und morgen you wil in eine speziale klinika por toxicos hospitalized esse. Esse in eine exotische marvellose platz mit pure mountain air und eternale snow around. Zum last, you shal placide rest und sicheremente relaxe!"

"Where esse diese platz, Otto?" pregunted Cabillot mucho suspiciose. Und additioned: "Dixit de veritas, bitte!"

Otto was hesitante. Before de speak, receded from der bed.

"Kabul, Herr inspector... Excuse mucho, aber de Europeane Polizei habe nicht bastante money por toi in eine Switzerlandia klinika hospitalize!"

Und aqui inspector Cabillot pronounced terribles blasphemante exclamationes in alles Europeanas linguas que man can repeat nicht.

2

Cabillot versus der malefiko Finnko

Was der jahro 2052. De Europeane Pax sich extended undisturbed from Portugallia zum Slovakkia, from Finlandia zum Cypro. Europa was indeed plus und plus grande. Aber ella was united und dat was essentiale. Germania was der leader country, in second platz come Franza, Nederlanda, Belgica, Luxemburga, Danelanda, Swedelanda, Finlandia, in terza platz come Italia, Espania, Ellenia, Portugallia. Dann come Polanda, Ungaria, Cekia, Slovakkia, Slovenia, Cypro und Turkelandia. Op bench reserva, come Grosse Britannia. In Brussel, der Europeane capitalcity, everydag millieros van eurofonzionarios, europolizeros, euroresercheros und eurosecretarias hardemente worked por make de Europeane machina werke. Finalmently, eine only lingua was gespoken: der Europanto. Partodo in Europa de Alto Europantico Instituto was cursos organizante so dat alles Europeanos citizenos Europanto als secunda lingua coudde speake. Die Europeanos fonzionarios necessite de pass every jahro eine Europanto examen. Diese jahro, Inspector Cabillot hadde estudied maxime scarcemente und was mucho embarassed mit der examen test:

How dixit in Europanto 'I love you' ?

A. Ich turbo toi
B. Ich amorante van toi
C. Me palpito por toi

Cabillot coudde chose nicht. Der professor ello regarded from der tabula mit mucho austeros eyos. Improviste, eine telefono dringed. Der professor responded, shaked de cabeza disappointado und dixit:

"Inspector Cabillot, suspende bitte seine test. Capitan What urgente necessite you. Cabillot souffled van relief und abandonned rapido de examen salle.

Capitan What was mucho furibonde. Ello walked from eine kant zum andere van seine buro, planting die bootes in der moquette.

"Merdenshit mundo!" was seine preferred imprecatione. "Quando, quando can moi in pension go! "

"Wat happen, Captain?" pregunted Cabillot.

"Lecture aquì!" dixit Capitan What, eine enveloppa aan Cabillot showingante. Cabillot opened der papier. Eine message mit gesticked journalo litteras was inside:

WIR HABE MANUEL BERLUSCONI KIDNAPPADO — POR SEINE LIBERATIONE WIR WANT DAT DIE FINNISCHE LINGUA REPLACE EUROPANTO IN EUROPA ALS ONLY LINGUA UND DAT SAUNA BECOME COMPULSORY IN IEDERE EUROPEANE CITY.

BASTA KERKES UND MOSQUES —
BASTA MIT OLDES RELIGIONES —
VIVA SAUNA!
VIVA EINE FINNISCHE EUROPA!
FINNKO BRUTAALO
ILLUSTRE NORDISCHE KRIMINAALO

P.S. If keine resposta in 15 dags, Ich shal Manuel Berlusconi evirate.

"Wie esse diese Finnko Brutaalo!" geshouted angryssimo Capitain What, mit eine bang van der hand der tabula shakerante.

"Ich habe scarce notizias, aber already ausculted van seine entreprises. Finnko Brutaalo esse eine fearable alternative terrorist. Sommige jahros ago ello maked bombe attaques aan engelse diktionarios publisheros in plurimos europeanos countries. Wanted impose finnische als universale lingua," responded Cabillot. Capitan What raised des poltronchair und regarded out des window der sonne sunsettante.

"Voilà eine mission por you, Inspector! Ich want que tu salvage Herr Berlusconi from diese dangerosissime kriminal! Es handelt aquì van der sexuale honour van eine volle Member State! Tu shal in Helsinki fahren und in contacto get mit Alko Liikko, unsere speziale scandinavo agent. Ello shal you assiste."

"Yesful, Capitan What!" dixit Cabillot und rapido got des buro out.

Cabillot gelanded in Helsinki in eine luminosa evening van

Junio. Eine strange stinkingante smell van vodka flotted op der aire. Cabillot thinked dat around er must esse eine distilleria.

"Hotel Torni, alstubitte!" dixit aan der taximano.

"Hotel Torni? Ah, ah, ah!" der taximano sinistrously sarcasticante snigged. Ello getrinked eine drop out van eine pocket bottella und departed in grosse speedesse. Out des taxi descendente, Cabillot was stupefacto, not to say gestonished. Partodo around, contra die muros, op der trotway und along des road was personas disruptamente drunken op der soil agonizantes.

"Helsinki in Junio esse eine permanente fiesta und almost esse compulsorio drunk dead sichself stone! Bienvenido in Helsinki Segnor! Ah, ah, ah!" Dixit der taximano grinnante und wroummed aweg. Der Hotel Torni was eine dark tower edificio. Inside, eine rossa moquette reminded eine strip-tease bar. Quando Inspector Cabillot entered in seine stanza, subitamente smelled eine forte tobacco smoke.

"Finallemente arrived!" exclamed eine vox in der shadow. Cabillot turned der lux interruptor. Op eine flowered poltronchair sitted eine fattissima dame, der pipe smokingante, die tittones als deflated ballones op der belly repliantes. Eine foot op der tabula keeped, so dat seine inguinale intimatesses visible was. Diese visione disgustante, aan Cabillot reminded italianse mortadella.

"Who esse you?" pregunted Cabillot annoyado.

"Alko Liikko, speziale scandinavo agente! Teine assistant aquì in Finlanda, naturallich!"

"Ich knew nicht dat you esse eine frau!" dixit mit surprisa Cabillot.

"Nor knew Ich!" replied die dame und addizionned: "aber maintenow, basta mit complimientos und lets starte unsere job. Open keine baggage. Wir immediate fahren aweg van

Helsinki."

"Porqué ?"

"Por die tracks te confonde und der enemy te disseminate!"

De fatte dama jumped van der poltronchair, dragged Cabillot out des stanza, out des hotel, inside eine autocarro und wroummed aweg in der blanca finnische nacht.

"Waar fahremos wir?" demanded Cabillot hurlante.

"Nach Nord! Direct in der nest des malefiko Finnko!" responded de fatte dama exaltada. Cabillot was hesitante, scarce convinced des efficacy van die eccentrique scandinave agent.

"Wir must rapido esto Finnko finden, alterwise poor Herr Berlusconi shal evirated esse! Und der prostitutione business shal disprofunde in recessione," dixit Cabillot mucho worried.

"Sans souci, kollega inspector. Wir shal op tempo arrive!" rassured Alko. Op ein moment distractione, smashed mit der autocarro eine couple rennadeer der strada crossingantes. Cabillot jumped terrorized from seine platz.

"Keine worry, Inspector! Ich esse well trained aan rennadeer smashing!" exclamed Alko Liikko mit eine infernale grin op seine mouth.

After longas horas van incessante travel, de autocarro stopped in eine forest, proximo eine lake. Cabillot remarked op der beechose shore eine wooden hutte van rubicond colour painted und eine kleine hutte next.

"Go inside und toi comfortable make!" dixit Alko Liikko. Cabillot entered in der hutte, sich allonged op der bed und presto was sleepingante. Quando rewakened, eine warme fog refilled de stanza. Someplatz burned eine stove. Dat was nicht der hutte waar Cabillot asleep hadde gefallen. Dat was de kleine hutte, de sauna hutte! Suddainely eine blanca, jelly masse sich approched und voluptuosemente him embraced. Kilos und kilos van fatte, transpirante meat op derl malfortunado Cabillot falled.

"Sweetissimo amor! Maintenow you esse tenfinally meine! Kisse, kisse me mucho! Ich siempre wanted eine continental lover!"

De fattissima Alko was sospirose gaspingante terwhile dat Cabillot inutile attempted de sich liberate. Overvicto by so tanta carne, Cabillot coudde respirationate nicht plus.

"Make me sex, meine cherido!" screamed van passion divampante Alko.

"Never! Esse virgin und pretende virgin remain!" protested Cabillot. Hours van combat beginned. Alko attempted in todas manieras Cabillot seduce, aber der heroische inspector resisted. In die pause, Cabillot adressed eine pray aan de Madonna und implored pardon por seine sinfulle life.

"Ich nicht even unterstande wat gender you esse! Male or female? Humane or animale?" objected Cabillot implorante.

"No matter der gender! Sophisticate persons can siempre diese details arrange! Kisse, bitte me kisse, querido!" insisted Alko und ex novo op Cabillot seine gelatinante ventrale obscenities squeezed.

Only quando Cabillot tenfinally fainted, Alko Liikko stopped. Ella got standing, marched over poor Cabillot, und spilled noch more wasser op der fumingante stove. Dann, por seine amoroso furor te calme, ella walked out und als eine grosse baleina, sich immerged in de placido laponische lake.

Tambien diese kind van sacrificios must eine Europeano polizei agente endure por seine noble mission te performe!

Diego Marani

Prisonero van de insatiable Alko, Cabillot remained dags und dags renclosed in der forest hutte.

"Ich shal you liberate only quando you sex moi make!" sentenced Alko, inconvincible.

"Forgette teine obsession und thinke aan unsere task! De ultimatum por de castratione van Herr Berlusconi esse more und more proximo!" implored Cabillot.

"Moi care absolute nicht! Tempo habe bastante. Make moi sex und dann you shal teine mission heroische accomplishe und mucho honour conquest!" Alko dixit, seine belly swingingante in front des disgusted inspector.

Por Cabillot in gut shape maintain, Alko compulsed him te masticate every dag fatte saucissones und multiple-egg-sabajone und te trinke seine speziale amor elizir: eine mix van bier, vodka, milko und chili pepperos. De only quiet moment por Cabillot was quando, jeder zwei dags, Alko nach de supermerkato him promenaded, in de proximo laponische village van Tuttimatti. Eine dag, in de queue aan der kassa expectante, Cabillot remarked eine hombre mit chinesische eyos. Hadde eine Chino appearance, aber laponische stature. Ello was carriyngante eine Mega Extra Large Pampers paquet in der chariotte.

"Strange! Ich habe never visto so grosse bambinos!" Cabillot dixit aan Alko.

"Lapponische bambinos can so grosse esse als ursos. Porqué ellos must van frost sich protecte in long arctische winter!" repliqued Alko.

"Ich esse convinced nicht!" insisted Cabillot und aan de exit followed mit die eyos dat bizarro hombre. Der laponische chino got op eine blaue jeep und fahred aweg along eine forest piste. Cabillot let sommige dags passe in de hutte saunante und aan Alko libido resistente. Dann, eine nacht, ello prepared seine evasion plan. Terwhile dat Alko was in der lake swimmingante, Cabillot replaced der amor elizir barrel mit eine nafta barrel. Quando Alko exit des wasser und toda nude und humide aan Cabillot sich approched voluminosa, Cabillot rapido kissed her und exclamede: "Teine elizier esse wonderbaar! Ich palpito por toi! Presto, trinke you tambien, meine libidinose amiga, trink! Und make rapido sexuale acrobaties!"

"Ah! Meine inspector! Tenfinally you surrender meine charm!" dixit Alko, und seine lips luxuriosa slappante, sich enflated der breast van air mit eine juicyoso kisso seine beloved inspector pumpingante. Cabillot crumbled onder die pulposos tittones remontantes und almost defainted van disgusto. Dann Alko grasped der barrel, opened der tappo und spilled into seine monstruose throat toda der nafta ohne even perceive der taste. Quando stopped, seine eyos flashante stared, eine grosse gurko made und op soil gefalled destroyed. Cabillot enrolled de fattona dame mit die snow chains dat founde in der hutte, dann charged her op der autocarro und wroummed nach der supermerkato. Ello wachted sommige tempo zum quando remarqued de blaue jeep arrivante. Als de precedente time, der hombre mit de chinesische eyos out des jeep descended und eine paquet van Pampers Mega Extra Large kauffed. Cabillot started der motor und prudently pursued de blaue jeep in der forest. After sommige kilometros, eine rubiconde hutte apparente was intra los trees. Cabillot let seine autocarro gut gehidden und sich slipped in der grass nach der hutte. Van der window coudde vision nicht, aber coudde entende die voices.

"Ich can nicht plus endure!" dixit eine hombre.

"Eine poquito pazience, Urmo! Presto shal todo over esse!" replied eine andere hombre.

"Ja, you dixit so! Aber you permane nicht aquì mit ello

todo der dag! Por terror, ello pisse todo der tempo in seine pantalon. Und Ich must siempre Pampers change! Finnko, Ich speel nicht plus! Wir subito evirate ello und gehe weg!"

Quando Cabillot entended dat name, eine tremor van angst grasped seine skin. Finnko! Der malefiko Finnko voilà esse! Und der pissingante prisonero dat die zwei hombres was speakingantes was surely Silvio Berlusconi! Cabillot permaned auscultante. Der voice van Finnko exploded in eine raged imprecatione:

"Keine protest, oder Ich shal teine kleine cervelle make explode! Wir combatte por de Finnische cause und wir must victoriosos esse! Subito enflamme de sauna por unsere prisonero!"

Cabillot rapido returned aan der autocarro waar Alko was stille dormingante.

Suddainely der Inspector hadde eine magnifica idea. Ello wachte dat die zwei hombres Herr Berlusconi in de sauna renclosed, dann pushed Alko out des autocarro und die snow chains removed. Siempre Alko from die feet tractante, mucho silentemente Cabillot sich approched des sauna, lentamente opened de portale, dragged Herr Berlusconi out und pushed Alko inside. Ohne forgette de perruque van Herr Berlusconi op der kopf van Alko te put. Dann de porta reclosed, op der autocarro Herr Berlusconi hissed und subito wroummed aweg. Op aquello same moment, der Inspector noticed in seine eurowatch dat der dag des ultimatum hadde gekomen. Aan der primera benzine stazion, der inspector telefoned aan Capitain What.

"Capitain What? Cabillot speakingante. Mission accomplida!"

"Maximos complimentos, Cabillot! Ich knewde dat Ich coudde over you reliable counte!"

Cabillot wroummed aweg mit seine autocarro und drived alles nacht nach Helsinki. Noch again, in der city entrante, ello smelled der same strange odour van vodka. Ello conducted Herr Berlusconi aan der Italianse Ambassade, waar der embassador bedanked muchissimo.

"Wir shal Herr Berlusconi op sex tourisme vacatione send. So dat ello shal recover presto healthemente well!" dixit der embassador de hand Cabillot shakerante. Cabillot salutante, left aan der embassador der restante paquet Pampers.

"In case Herr Berlusconi hadde noch sommige pissose crisis," explained Cabillot.

"Und forgette nicht de skin pommade por inflamed buttockes!" recommanded again der inspector.

Before de go zuback nach Brussel, Cabillot decided dat deserved eine gut glass trink, der successo des operazion celebrante. So der inspector entered eine bar und commanded:

"Eine gefrozen vodka alstubitte!"

"Mucho sorry desolate, Segnor. Wir habe keine vodka plus. Esse de einde des summer und wir habe getrinked alles."

"Alles?"

"Alles vodka van Finlandia!"

"Ah! Dann give moi eine whiskio!"

"Desolate Segnor, wir habe tambien todo wiskio getrinked!"

"Eine bier?"

"Bier? Allow me regarde..." der barmano opened der frigor.

"No, keine bier nicht plus. Habe only multiple-egg-sabajone left!"

Perplexed und relinquishente, Cabillot trinked seine multiple-egg-sabajone. Aber respirante der frische air nocturno, noticed again dat odour van vodka. Maxime strange: keine vodka in de bar, aber vodka odour all around. Was truly somecosa strange in dat pays. Mumblante, el returned al autocarro und drivingante aweg along des empty stradas van Helsinki, noticed mucho people zum de harbour meetingante.

Op der same momento, in der hutte des forest, Finnko was de radio auscultante.

"Radiojournalo van medianacht" dixit der radioman und continued: "Finlandia habe internazionale aid demanded porqué totale run out van alle alkolische trinkes. Eine Rode Kross cisterne ship van antifrost full esse vanout Hamburgo departingante por primeros secoursos aan Finlandia apporte. Finlandesos onder shock, van abstinency sufferentes, wait der ship camped along des Baltische coast. Finnko turned der interruptor off und mit mucho seriose voice dixit:

"Urmo, der ultimatum esse over. Take der knife! Wir castrate Berlusconi!"

"Tenfinally!" exclamed Urmo die hands rubbingante. Dann eine sauvage cry pulverized de silenciouse laponische nacht und maked der placido lake ripple van terror.

Mucho tempo passed. Der automne arrived und der winter tambien. Eine frigide morning van Jenero, in seine buro entrante, Cabillot founde op seine tabula eine postalcarte vanout Finlandia. De image showed eine blanco und paxfulle landscape. Op der back was gewritten:

"Danke aan you, meine sexuale life hadde eine totale cambio. Maintenow esse Ich eine real dama. Ich shal forever toi remembrare, Inspector! Kissos, Alka Seltzer. (Ja, now habe ich gemarried mit Herr Seltzer, eine wunderbaro und mucho macho y rudo swedische timbermanno!).

3

Cabillot und de greeka myopa cyclopa

Eine Augusto postmeridio, Cabillot was in seine officio eine crossverba in Europanto solvente. Out des window, under eine unhabitual sonne splendente, de city gasped van calor. Zweideca vertical: "Esse greeko, esse blanco und masticable", quatro litteras. Cabillot was nicht so bravo in crossverbas. Seine boss obliged crossverbas make por seine brainose cervelle in exercizio keep, aber dat postmeridio inspector Cabillot was mucho somnolento. Wat esse greeko, esse blanco und masticable? May esse eine glace-cream? No, dat esse italiano aber greeko nicht. Und man slappe, nicht masticate. Cabillot slowemente closed die eyos und falled sleepingante op seine buro. Der telefono dringante presto him rewakened.

"Hallococco! Cabillot speakingante!" responded mucho groggy.

"Aquì Capitain What! Come subito in meine officio!"

"Yesful, meine Capitain!" responded Cabillot out van der door sich envolante.

Capitan What was muchissimo nervoso der map des Europa op der wall regardante und seine computero excitatissimo consultante.

"Cabillot! Wir habe diese messagge op der computero received! Regarde alsyoubitte!"

Cabillot sich approched des monitor und lectured:

BASTA MIT DER LATINO ALFABETO! VIVA DER GREEKO ALFABETO!

OP 15 AUGUSTO AT MEDIANACHT ICH SHAL TEINE COMPUTEROS

SABOTAGE UND ALLES DIE U.E. DOCUMENTOS SHAL IN MORSE ALFABETO GEWRITTEN!

FRICTOS KALAMAROS

ACCOMPLISHADOS ELLENICOS TUPAMAROS

G.A.F.

"Inspector, you know who esse Frictos Kalamaros?" pregunted Capitain What.

"Keine idea!" confessed der inspector.

"Esse der machtig boss des G.A.F., die Greekos Alfabeticos Fundamentalistos! Inspector, wir can allow nicht dat der Lisbon Treaty in der Morse alfabeto verchanged esse! Dann, voilà eine mission por you, Inspector! Ich want you go nach Greeklandia und enquest. Reporte moi plus soon dat possible! Remembra dat todag esse alnoch 13 Augusto! Habe zwei dag tempo, Inspector!" dixit Captain What de hand aan Cabillot shakerante und seine kopf pattingante.

"Ah! Before dat departe, passe alsyoubitte by unsere cervelloso secreto laboratorio por sommige speziale weapones!" additionned der Captain und sitted zuback in seine poltronchair. Cabillot mumblingante descended mit der liftor zum minus 30 level, waar der laboratorio van Mr.Genius was.

"Salve, Mr. Genius. Wat habe for moi?"

"Ah, Inspector! Ich was teine coffret preparante! Here esse eine speziale spray bottella por muttones frighten und aweg keep!"

"Die muttones? Porqué die muttones?" repliqued Cabillot mucho perplexo.

"Man never know wat can happene. Yesterdag die vaches folles, morgendag die muttones... Animals can dangerosos esse!" responded placidly Mr. Genius

"Und wat else?" pregunted Cabillot in der coffret regardante.

"Ah! Aquì tambien eine cuisine book spezial por sardine receptes!"

"Ah! Sardine receptes... Und wat for?"

"For sardines te cuisine! Sardines esse mucho healthy, inspector und er esse mucho fosfore inside die gut esse por brainose cervello!" dixit Mr. Genius mucho convincente.

Inspector Cabillot taked seine coffret und walked aweg de kopf shakerante. Diese eveningo out des avioplano in Athenai descendente, Inspector Cabillot knowde nicht yet van waar te beginne seine enquest. So decided de beginne eine aperitivo trinkante und sitted aan eine terrasse in der centro van der city.

"Ouzo?" pregunted der waitero.

"Ouzo!" responded Cabillot in perfecto greeko.

Cabillot was tranquilo seine Ouzo sippante quando eine immensa figura approched und sitted next him. Der inspector almost evanished van scare regardante de gigantesqua dama dat mit seine jellifluo buttockones, der fulle divano occuped. Zwei gorillische legs opened in front des inspector obscurando der sonne sunsettingante. Eine hand als grosse als eine vache descended van der top des monstruosa figura und shaked der fragile hand des Inspector. Cabillot der hand retracted horrificatissimo und jumped screamingante, quando remarked dat de dama over him prospectante, behinde van eine monoculo, eine only eyo hadde. Was eine monoculose dame.

"Eine only, eine poquito myope, aber blaue!" exclamed de

gigantesca figura coquettemente, seine eyo in vitrina mit der finger pointante.

"Enchantada! Meine name esse Psychodramma. Ich esse eine cyclopa, far aweg relative van Polyphemos, der one from Odissea!" ella additionned smilingante.

"Enchantado! Inspector Cabillot, van de Europeane Polizei, Service des Bizarre Affairs!" marmotted der inspector.

"Ich know porqué you aqui esse!" whispered die dama aan der auricular des inspector. Cabillot mucho embarassado sich retracted nach der wall quando der waitero approched irritado und mit fastidiosa vox dixit:

"Perdone, aber aqui los vagabundos und los cyclopes esse admitted nicht! Ich must you invite teine cyclope aweg te conducte, anders Ich shal de Hellenikà Polizeià appelle!"

"Aber esse meine cyclope nicht! Ich habe keine cyclope!" protested Cabillot. Suddenamente die gigantica dama mit eine hit des hands todas die tabulas und die umbrellose parasols des bar aweg projected und muchissimo imbestialized screamed aan der waitero:

"Maleducated, bruto und cyclopophobo! (Eine van de worste greekos insultones). Tu accepte cattos, doggos, Albanesos, even Turcos und Italianos aber no accepte Cyclopos! Cyclopos esse mucho plus greek dann you! Wir esse die primeros, eche greekos! Ich shal des Internationale Cyclope Rights Tribunale addresse. Er est keine Apartheid in Greeklandia!"

"Calme, madama, calme" dixit Cabillot conciliante, de dama por seine tunique pullingante. "Gehemos eine promenada te make!" proposed der inspector.

Cabillot managed die gigantica dama nach de Akropolis te tracte. De kopf inclinante por under die columnas des Partenon te passe, die cyclopa beginned te raconte:

"Ich know how Frictos Kalamaros capture!" murmured die cyclopesse.

"Trulymente?" repliqued Cabillot.

"Frictos Kalamaros esse eine tycone richissimo. Ello live alles tempo op seine luxuoso yacht, de 'Makako' und never disbarque op land. Aber ich habe eine idea por him attracte in eine trap! Frictos Kalamaros esse mucho gourmando van kalamaros frictos. Ello can tons of kalamaros masticate!"

"Go adelante!" dixit Cabillot.

"Wir shal op der journalo eine advertisemento publicare mit propagande eine speziale verkauffe sale van frische kalamaros op meine piccola islanda."

"Tu habe eine islanda?"

"Alles cyclopes habe eine! Esse eine question van status. Cyclopes ohne islanda esse keine cyclopes!"

"Ah! Bitte continue!" encouraged Cabillot de dama.

"So, was expliquante dat Kalamaros shal certainly come te regarde. Mucho curiose por kalamaros. Wir let ello approche, dann Ich shal eine blok van rock op seine bootship projecte und Kalamaros adieu, farewell, basta, finito!" exclamed surexcitada de cyclopa.

"Waar esse teine islanda?" pregunted suspicioso Cabillot.

"Come tomorgen aan der Pyreos harbour! Wir shal mit meine bootship daar gehen! In der meantempo, Ich shal verkauffe eine hondred kilos kalamaros por unsere trap plus efficace make!"

Der morgen after Cabillot arrived aan Pyreos, als promised. Psychodramma was op der pierpont expectante mit eine containero full kalamaros grouillosos swarmingantes, mucho appetitose apparente.

"Waar esse teine bootship?"

"Hier!" dixit de cyclopa. Mit eine hand taked der containero und mit eine kick des piedone renversed der pierpont over der wasser, dann sitted op.

"Attenzio zum departe!" cried Psychodramma. "Inspector, graspe alsyoubitte meine shoulder por der horizonte te inspecte und die rocks moi signale. Meine vista esse sfortunately mucho deficiente!"

Mit eine olive arbor roamingante, de cyclopa directed seine very speciale bootship nach der alto sea. Cabillot over seine shoulder was der horizonte pointilliste scannerante. After eine kleine hora van navigatione, ellos hadde quatro times out des bootship gefallen und op eine bank van sand gestranded. Fortunatamente, die kalamaros got gelossen nicht. Nach der eveningo ellos tenfinally disbarqued op eine piccola islanda ohne arbors und full van muttones.

"Liebe you meine islanda?" pregunted Psychodramma der containero op der plage deponente.

"Prefero Seychellas..." objected critische Cabillot.

"In die Seychellas, esse muttones nicht!" puntualized de cyclopa terwhile mit der pierpont eine bungalovo op der playa was buildante. Er was indeed eine multitasking cyclopa.

"Diese nacht sleepe aquì. Tomorgen, quando die journalos shal publicados esse, ich think dat Kalamaros shal presto aquì arrive!" dixit Psychodramma und falled sleepingante, als eine diesel motor snoringante. In der meantempo die muttones sich interessed aan die boots van inspector Cabillot. Superalles die strings, ellos liebed mucho de taste. Cabillot rapido opened seine coffret und sprayed arounde der speziale produkto van Mr. Genius. Subitamente de muttones retracted und sich regrupped beelantes op der back des cyclopa.

Diego Marani

Quando come der morningo, de cyclopa in der sleep dreamingante, ohne attentione, mit eine piedone Cabillot in der sea pushed. Der ispector almost suffoqued in der wasser. Pantingante, Cabillot was sich rewarmante aan die rayones des sonne levante. De fulle body scratchante por dolorose contusione, ello decided along des playa sich promenade, quando op der horizonte eine zwarte, menaceante bootship remarqued.

"Psychodramma, rewake presto! Habemos eine visita!"

De cyclopa sich turned imposante und alles muttones op seine back relaxantes maked op air volantes.

"Ah, ah! Es worked! Frictos Kalamaros falled in unsere trap! Presto! Inspector, make semblante der kalamaros verkauffer te esse!" cried de cyclopa alles kalamaros op el pierpont renversante.

"Ich shal behindo diese mountain moiself hidde und op teine signalo eine blok van rock op de 'Makako' projecte!"

In der meantempo, op der 'Makako', Frictos Kalamaros was in seine bathtub relaxante, van champagne sichself aspergente.

"Ah, ah! Tomorgen todos die computeros des U.E. shal in alfabeto Morse write und nomanno shal nicht plus able esse der Lisbon Treaty de lecture!"

Kalamaros taked out van eine bowle sommige kalamaros und los masticated mucho piggemente, der champagne van seine bathtub sippingante, while seine grosso und gorilloso belly scratchingante.

"Pedro! Necessito more kalamaros! Quanto distance por de islanda van de speziale verkauffe?"

Pedro, der esclavo van Kalamaros runned haletante op der

41

deck.

"Maestro, de islanda esse op proxima vista!"

"Ah, dann gehemos presto!"

Kalamaros stande out des bathtub, sich wrapped in eine zwarte peignoir mit eine yellowe "K" op der back und eine grosse burpo in der matinale air released.

Op de islanda, Cabillot was frenetico expectante. Ello hadde eine pankarte op der pierpont gefixed: 'Kalamaros Speziale Verkauffe — Ultime dag'. Der Inspector wachte paziente dat der Makako proximo esse. Quanto opportune momento, ello cried fortemente:

"Schoote!"

Psychodramma distached eine blok van marble vanout des mount und es projected nach der bootship. Aber because van seine vista deficiente, missed flagrantemente der target.

"Megamerdenshit! (Tipische greeka exclamatione) Es missed! Maintenow dat krimilano shal nos bombarde mit seine terrible weapona!"

"Wat esse seine terrible wepona?" Cabillot hadde only der tempo de pose der pregunta porqué subito eine tempesta van sardinas down from der sky op de islanda falled. De muttones beelantes was partodo escapingantes. Cabillot was in die sardines tot die knees sprofundante und die muttones op kopf jumpantes por not submerge in diese avalanche van fish. Eine insupportable stink infected der air.

"Presto, throw noch eine andere blok, anders de Makako shal schoote again!" ordered der inspector.

"Mucho willingante! Aber wat happen if miss noch again?"

"Momento! Ich shal op teine shoulderos climbe und you directe in der cannonamento des blok! So dat miss der target nicht!" proposed Cabillot.

"Gut! Pronto?"

"Pronto! Plus aan west, maintenow plus nach south, plus low... Gut! Now! Schoote!"

Psychodramma eine mastodontische marble blok projected in der air. Man ausculted eine longo sifflemento, dann eine torpedose blastamento mit fire und fumigationes. Der Makako was in der sea sprofundante.

"Victoria!" exclamed Psychodramma triumphante.

Far aweg, in der medio des sea, Kalamaros und Pedro inside eine zwarte canotto was imprecantes.

"No finish aquì!" cried Kalamaros seine hand rageoso agitante nach der distante islanda van Psychodramma.

"Muchas bedankes! You was splendida shouteresse!" dixit Cabillot de cyclopa complimentante, und additionned:

"Maintenow wir must de victoria celebrate. Just por hazard, habe Ich mit moi eine sardine cuisine recepte book!" Cabillot und Psychodramma prepared eine speziale banquet mit sardines und kalamaros. Todos die cyclopos des Aegeano Sea was invited zum party mit seine muttones. Man maked mucha fiesta, alles de nacht durante canzones cantantes und mucho vino drinkantes.

El morningo suivante, aan el Pyreos harbour was una telefon box encircled van cattos und nomanno knewde porqué. Inspector Cabillot was inside telefonante.

"Hallococco, Capitain What? Cabillot speakingante. Mission accomplida! De machtig Frictos Kalamaros esse K.O. der Lisbon Treaty esse salvaged!"

"Congratulationes, inspector! Ich shal toi propose por eine medal!"

"Keine medal, Capitain What! Eine promotion suffice! Aber aquì esse noch eine problema..."

"Wat problema?" pregunted Capitain What.

"Meine amiga cyclopa..." dixit Cabillot regardante along des pierpont Psychodramma sobbante und commotionned suspirante.

"Esse keine job possible por eine cyclopa in de Europeane Polizei?"

"Eine cyclopa? Esse you crazy horse become, inspector! Er esse keine job por eine cyclopa in de Europeane Polizei!"

"Ella me helped mucho! Eine preziose investigatoresse!"

Op der andere side des line, Capitain What was silente. Cabillot insisted.

"Ella esse mucho gut educated und gentile. Wat plus, ella can maxime useful esse, Capitain What!"

"You winningante, inspector! Ich shal teine cyclopa enrole! Aber keine promotion und keine medal! Unterstuddo?"

"Unterstuddo, Capitain What! You habe eine goldene corazon!"

Zuback in Brussel, sommige dags after, in seine officio Cabillot was again crossverba in Europanto solvente.

"Psychodramma, wat esse greeko, esse blanco und masticable? Quatro litteras?"

"De Feta! Wat anders!" responded Psychodramma. Ella was eine wollen pull por seine muttones knittingante terwhile eine greeke tragedia op Iphone auscultante.

"Optime Psychodramma! Ich knewde que you maxime useful por de Europeane Polizei esse!" exclamed Cabillot

Diego Marani

mucho satisfacto.

Voilà how happened que der Europeane Polizei seine primera cyclopa enroled.

4

Cabillot versus de Demente Bovine Frakzion

In seine Brussel officio, Inspector Cabillot regarded de rain out des window while thinkante aan quanto tempo und quanto work necessited por Europa tefinally united make. Plurimos jahros ello hadde worked in de Europeane Polizei und muchos progressos was performed. Aber noch mucho permaned te make. Porqué before de make Europa, one shoudde de Europeanos make. Und es was keine Europeano in Europa yet. Es was Franzosos, Hispanicos, Italianos, Germanicos, Slovenos, Boemos, Turcos, Polonesos und manige anderes, aber keine Europeano. Inspector Cabillot was der unique, autentique Europeano. In seine fantasia navigante, Cabillot hadde der telefono dring entended nicht. Dringed desde eine lot van tempo.

"Hallococco Cabillot! Who speakante?" ello responded.

"Capitain What! Who anders want que toi call! Wat was makeante? No ausculted der telefono?"

"Excusazio, Capitain What. Ich was thinkante..."

"Dann come here thinke! Porqué wir habe eine abjectissimo problema zum solve!"

Inspector Cabillot dressed seine blaue officiero jacket und exit des office. Capitain What was siempre eine poquito harshe. Aber ello was eine honest hombre, mucho serious und traballador. Ello was eine olde British secreto agent. In der facts ello was still presentemente eine British secreto agent des MI5. Aber so secreto dat nomanno in Grosse Britannia remembered van ello. Dat esse why ello decided de enrole in de Europeane Polizei, mit der sincero hope dat London remembered ello, repented de ello habe neglected und tenfinally proposed eine excitantissima mission. Aber toch, nomanno ello remembered. So why Capitain What permaned in de Europeane Polizei.

"Make youself commodo, herr inspector!" dixit Capitain What aan Cabillot eine kleine stool indiquante. Dann crossed die fingers over de tabula und eine letter aan Cabillot showante, speaked adelante:

"Inspector, lecture bitte diese message." Cabillot lexit:

BASTA MIT DE HUMANA ARROGANZE!
DE HUMANA EUROPA SHAL PRESTO OVER!
VIVA DE BOVINE EUROPA!

D.B.F. (Demente Bovine Frakzion)

"Esse eine fantasiose toch amusante joke!" snorted Cabillot.

"Esse keine joke. Esse plus dann true. Die madde bovinos van all Europa united in Grosse Britannia und last nacht taked der power in London!"

"You mean dat op diese momento in Downing street..."

"Esse eine bovine regime! Todos britannicos esse terrorized! Die bovinos ellos capture und ellos enfermed in die cowstables als krieg prisonieros!" shouted Capitain What mit seine eyos out des kopf.

"Und wat say de Queen?" pregunted Cabillot.

"De Queen say 'muuuu!' Porqué esse eine milk vache ella tambien und sich name Margaritta Primera. Elisabetha per contre esse enfermed in de royale cowstable!" exclamed Capitain What mucho excitado.

"Unterstando... So, wat esse meine orders, Herr Capitain?" pregunted Cabillot bastante worried.

"Infiltre die vaches, finde eine maniera por ellas concentrate alles in de Wimbledon stadium und quando esse ready, send moi eine signalo. Wir shal from Normandy eine rokette over Wimbledon shoote und destroy die revolucionarias bovinos once por ever! Welcomido in operatio 'Omaha Beef' herr inspector!"

"Aber, Capitain What! How can Ich die bovinos infiltrare!"

"Esse teine businesso, inspector! Esse oder non esse der primero inspector des Europeane Polizei? Dann arrange youself. Und beste fortune!"

"Can Ich meine assistant, Frau Psychodramma mit moi take?"

"Yesful. Und forgette nicht de passe by Herr Genius por die equipment!" dixit encore Capitain What de porta noisemente shuttando.

Inspector Cabillot taked die liftor, exit in eine longo corridor neonico luminoso und frapped aan die porta van seine assistant. Frau Psychodramma was noch eine wool covertura knittingante por seine muttones, aan die radio eine sirtaki jam session auscultante.

"Habe nostalgy van teine islanda?" pregunted Cabillot.

"No. Aber esse eine poquito worried por meine muttones. Winter esse rapido arrivante..." responded melanchonica Psychodramma.

"Tu shal presto eine andere islanda visit. Und de novo Ich necessite teine helpo"

"Meine helpo?" repeated de cyclopa.

"Tu esse eine experte in muttones, esse you?"

"Grandemente!"

"Thinke dat you can manage mit bovinos tambien?"

"Equallemente! Esse tranquilo. Alles wat op quatro feet stande, can Ich facile handle!"

"Gutissimo! Dann, take teine affaires und gehemos. Wir departe por Grosse Britannia!"

Antes des departe es was noch eine stop te make by Herr Genius, de cervelloso researchero des secreto polizei laboratorio. Cabillot und seine assitant so descendend nach el minus 30 level van de Polizei Tower.

"Ah, herr Cabillot! Ich was you expectante. Hier esse teine magic box mit alles you necessite por teine missione!" dixit Herr Genius terwhile dat eine gigantesque plastic container in front van Cabillot opened.

"Hier esse eine Osborne bullo disguise." Herr Genius desrolled op der floor eine immense plastic blacke bullo disguise als die Osborne Sherry publicitarios panels.

"Wat esse for?" pregunted Cabillot almost furibonde por diese useless gadgettos.

"You go in eine bovine country, go you? So eine bullo esse siempre useful!"

"Ah!" exclamed Cabillot perplexo.

"Und dann habe wir eine echte leather balle!" continued herr Genius aan Cabillot showingante eine fuss-balle ballone.

"Und wat esse diese balle for?" insisted Cabillot

"Esse presto der Mundial Fuss-balle Championnado und

wat plus, you go in de fuss-balle homelandia. How can you ohne ballone stay?"

"Unterstando, unterstando," dixit Cabillot mucho doubtvolle.

Die container reclosante, herr Genius mucho calorosamente saluted:

"Gutte fortuna, Cabillot! Que viva der victory des Europa, siempre!"

Cabillot nodded mit eine snort und der container aan seine assistante indiquante, dixit

"Alstubitte, Psychodramma, can you diese coffret transporte?" Psychodramma ohne fatigue der grosse boxe op seine shoulder deposed.

Cabillot und Psychodramma departed eine radioso soleado morning nach der harbour van Calais. Ellos was planningante op ferryboat travel, porqué Eurotunnel can cyclopes nicht embarque. People die zwei agentes encounteringantes, was mucho shocked voyante aquello strange couple: eine myopa cyclopa mit eine containero op der shoulder escorted by eine polizero agente in de blaue uniforme van die Europeane Polizei. Op der motorweg die camioneros los claxonne allegros und across die fields sommige dogs los pursued barkingantes. Aber zum Calais arrivantes, keine ferrybarca accepted de los charge. De cyclopa surpassed die allowed measures por encombrantes transportes, tambien op navale cargo. So die zwei amigos decided de traverse die Manche Channel op feet: Psychodramma in der sea walkingante, der containero over die waves pushante, und Cabillot aan seine shoulders solidamente gripped. Es was eine mytische spectaculo, in de rubiconde atmosphera des sonne sunsettingante, eine cyclopa in der middle des sea progressante. Seagulles, baleines und mackerellos, alles natura stopped by diese visione fulminated. Once op de andere side des Channel, die zwei agentes sich hidde behinde die witte rocks und wachted der morningo mucho watchfully vigilantes.

Partodo in Grosse Britannia die bovinos hadde der power forte in seine grip. Die routes was patrolled by speziale guardias: mucho feroces zwarte Ardense bovinos. Cabillot und Psychodramma coudde travel only across die countryside. Terwhile nach London travelantes, ellos encountered plurimas farms waar britannicos paysanos enfermed was in die staples criantes, als animales labourantes.

Quando in London, de nacht hadde fallen. Cabillot und Psychodramma sich hidde in eine metro station. Die bovinos liked der metro nicht und so daar was eine safe platz te permane.

"Wat make maintenow?" pregunted Psychodramma eine poquito discouraged

"Wir habe der task de renclose die bovinos in de Wimbledon stadium. Necessite eine maniera finde por diese task absolve..." responded Cabillot mucho sombre conjecturante.

"Aber how?" pregunted depressedly Psychodramma.

"Know nicht yet. Aber als wir in London esse, wir must profit take und fun habe. Diese abend wir shal out gehen por eine glass bier! Presto disguise youself mit der Osborne bullo. Ich shal hidde over teine shoulder, unter die disguisamiento."

Aquello eveningo, eine grosse Osborne bullo came out des Piccadilly Circus metro station und sich mixed aan die bovine crowd in die streets promenante.

"Wat eine bullo!" exclamed algunas jonge bovinos nach der disco gehentes. Esse true que Psychodramma in black gedressed made eine mucho elegante bullo. By Leicester

Square, de cyclopa entered in eine pub und ordered eine shandy.

"Not eine shandy, stupida! Tu esse eine mucho masculino bullo! Tu drinke bitter bier oder whiskio!" whispered Cabillot aan der neck des cyclopa grasped.

"Eine doppel whiskio, alsyoubitte!" sich corrected Psychodramma.

"Gut!" dixit Cabillot, und pursued: "Now Ich habe eine idea. Tu must fuss-balle talk und mucho polemico esse! Unterstuddo? Wir must push die bovinos aan fuss-balle play!"

"Unterstuddo!" declared Psychodramma eine poquito altered by der doppel whiskio.

Eine couple bovinos was proxime chatterantes. Psychodramma so maked seine primera bovine avance:

"Olà! Wat beautifulle juventus! Wat esse you from?"

Die bovinos beginned te smile, in der meantempo inter ellas whisperantes.

"Wir esse germanicas, plus precisely, bavarisches..."

"Ah! Die Bayern Munich fuss-balle equipo! Und die charmante teutonicos bovinose muchachas! Was altime meine passion in Benidorm germanicas blonde bovinose muchachas entertain op der sea playa! Esse op holidag in Engelandia?" repliqued Psychodramma preguntante

"Wir esse mit die Occupazion Bovine Army hier arrived. Und you?"

"Ich esse van de Hispanica Bovina Brigada "Bovinos sin frontera". Wir esse voluntarios die partodo in der mundo rush ter helpo des bovine race in distress!"

"Oh! Muchos complimentos!" exclaimed die germanisches bovinos impressed.

"Diese nacht wir gehemos chinese food masticate! Want nos accompany?" proposed dann mucho impertinently de plus beautifulle des quatro bovinose muchachas.

"Porqué nicht?" responded Psychodramma mit seine performance mucho reassured und addizionned: "Eine bullo mit quatro bovinose muchachas esse bastante respectable!"

De Soho chinese restaurante por bovinos only hadde eine mucho disgusteful menu van fried oder steamed cantonese soya und andere revoltante herbale panoplia. Never der minus, Psychodramma masticated courageousemente die verdura.

"You jonge bovinos van todag esse mucho more intelligente dann nostra generatio" insinuated Psychodramma nonchalante und insisted:

"Aber no esse yet bastante moderne, nicht bastante insolente! By exemplo, esse presto in die humana Europa de Mundial fuss-balle Championnado und aquì in bovine Engelandia nobody thinked de show aan der mundo dat die bovinos nicht inferior des hombres esse und dat can mucho well fuss-balle play op der same level van primera division championnado!"

"Esse true!" exclamed die more entreprenante bovino.

"Porqué not organize eine championnado?" suggested eine andere bovino.

"Yesful! Eine authentiquo bovine championnado! Mit quatro feet wir shal certainly mucho more goals make dann die hombres mit zwei!"

"Aan de Bovine Mundiale fuss-balle Championnado!" dixit Psychodramma eine toast makeante mit eine glass van tea.

"Prosit!" responded die teutonicos bovinos.

Op diese moment, eine olde bovine frau approched des gruppe.

"Who esse diese foreignero?" pregunted mucho suspectful.

"Toro Pepito Lopez y Sanchez y Gutierrez y tambien un poquito Hernandez, Caudillo Maximo des Bovinos sin Frontera. Por you serve, Madama!" dixit Psychodramma eine elegante curtesy bow makeante.

"Ah, enchanted. Ich esse die Generalissima Frau Bismarck, des secreto service!" responded die bovine frau.

"Bismarck? De one van die steak?" demanded Psychodramma muchissimo undelicate.

"Exactamente! Moi und meine familie esse hier porqué wir want dat nicht more out van nostra carne man make bifsteaks!" repliqued mucho bitterly aber frankly die generalissima.

"You esse rightful! Basta mit der bovine massacre!" approved Psychodramma.

"Ja, basta! Wir shal die humanos submitte aan unsere power!" dixit de Generalissima.

"Justemente, how thinke de humana race subjugate?" pregunted mucho subdola Psychodramma.

"Hier in Grosse Britannia wir submit humanos aan re-education programmas: wir oblige hombres de trinke tea mit zitrone und ohne milk, de masticate chicken, oder die frogs, oder die fish aber keine quadrupede carne!" explained Frau Bismarck.

"Und if ellos no obey? doubted Psychodramma.

"Wir make dann torquemada!" dixit de Generalissima seine witte, glaciale eyos horridamente rollante.

"So you necessite mucha propaganda make in favor des bovina race!" interjected embarrassed Psychodramma van subject changeante. Dann pursued expliquante:

"Ich was juste aan die jonge mademoiselles eine idea suggestante por eine grande bovine sportiva manifestatio die show aan der volle mundo wat nos bovinos esse able te make!"

Psychodramma explained aan die generalissima Bismarck seine fuss-balle projecto und die olde frau showed mucho interest.

Durante die followantes eveningos, again und again, Psychodramma in Osborne bullo disguised transited from eine pub zum de andere mit Cabillot op de shoulder gehidden, propagandante de idea van eine bovine fuss-balle championnado. Op seine side, de generalissima tambien, mucho entousiastica supported de projecto und beginned forme fuss-balle equipos, initiallemente in Hyde Park sich entrainantes. Every pays hadde seine equipo: es was Germania, Belgica, Hispania, Englandia, Galleslandia, Scotlandia, Eirlandia, Nederlandia, Polandia, Boemia, Portugallia, Danelandia und so on.

"Aber wir necessite eine balle! Wir habe keine balle! Wir cannot play mit eine bovine leather balle!" remarqued eine morningo die generalissima.

"Keine worry. Hier esse die balle!" repliqued Psychodramma die ballone van Herr Genius op der grass kickante.

"Van leather frog! Mucho delicate por bovine hoof."

"Tenemos eine balle!" shouted die playadoras excitatissimas und beginned mit quatro feet de balle over der campo te dribble.

Die qualification matches presto started. Every domingo in die plurimos stadiums van Grosse Britannia, grandes masses van bovinos exultantes assisted aan die primeros bovinos soccer matches des historia. Desde subito Germania nationale bovine equipo sich revealed eine van die beste equipos playantes. Psychodramma was partodo requested als referee, tambien porqué ella was alnoch in black gedressed. Ter ende, die dag des finale approched. Germania und Englandia were sich confrontantes por der title des champion des bovine mundo.

Diese eveningo, hidden in der Piccadilly metro, Cabillot und Psychodramma prepared die ultimes details des operazio 'Omaha Beef'.

"While que you arbitre der match, Ich shal hide in eine telefonbox next des Wimbledon stadium. Op media hora past nine Ich shal telefone aan Capitain What. You wachte one minuto dann escape out des stadium. Unterstuddo?" explained Cabillot aan de cyclopa.

"Unterstuddo!" repliqued ella.

Es was eine memorable nacht. Alles die luminarias flamboyantes, brillante van eclat maked de whole Wimbledon stadium. Die supporteros in der stadium acclamantes hadde noch some scaramouchade mit de Bovine Police engaged. Sommige bovinos hooliganos was presto brutalmente deported, por der sake des gut course des match. Die zwei equipos was op der campus aligned, Germania mit witte und Englandia mit rosso uniforme. Die nationale anthems solemnemente resounded, dann der initiale whistle. Germania presto taked der lead mit eine counterattack, aber die englanda defense pronto responded adequately. De match was played supratodo in der medio campo, signal que die zwei equipos was still each andere estudiante. Psychodramma correctamente arbitred, seine unico eyo aan der time panel sometimes tournante. Eine quarter hora passed van balanced play, mit rare und unefficace shoots nach die goals, quando improvisto die englando centroadelante playador die balle mit eine cross received, zwei germanicos dribbled und acrobaticamente in der net sich propulsed, eine robusto goal strikeante. In exstatica raptura. De public van seine seat jumpante maked eine megalo hurlo in der nocturno sky roboante. Was preciso media hora past nine. Aber die cyclopa was eine myopa one. Ella read op el time panel nine 'o cloque. In der meantempo, in der telefonbox expectante, Cabillot regarded seine watch und die exit des stadium mucho worried. Donde Psychodramma was? Ten last, mit mucha anxiety in der corazon, der inspector grasped der receiver. May esse dat Psychodramma van eine andere exit escaped. Dann der inspector dialled der secreto numero und dixit: "Operatio Omaha Beef, fire!"

In seine bunker op eine normandische playa, Capitain What admired der starred sky noch eine time, dann seine cigarette under de boot smashed und position taked at seine megalo eurotunnel cannon. After zwei minutos over der London sky die celestiale black subito enflammed become. Eine grosse explosione resounded, de soil shakerante. Aber de Wimbledon stadium was noch intacto. Op der same momento, in der stadium die bovinos rushed nach der exit, mooantes van terror. Aber Psychodramma pronto obstructed der passage, mit Osborne hornos chargeante any bovino approchante.

"Der target missed! Presto correcte der shoot!" reclamed Cabillot zum telefono, siempre de stadium exit inutile scannerante. After zwei minutos, again eine rubiconde cloud vamped in der sky und eine andere explosion de soil smashed. Aber noch de stadium was intacto.

"Donde pointe? Missed tambien again! Correcte der shoot!" was Cabillot al telefono yellingante. Op der pitch, Psychodramma coudde resist nicht more. Ella caramboled out und mit eine starke kick over der wall, maked die entrance portale crumble als eine quakeose strike. Die bovinos was interne trapped. De cyclopa in der darke smoke distinguente,

Cabillot mucho relieved signale maked aan Psychodramma de escape und join ello outside, quando ex novo eine volcanico roar de celestiale dark fractured und over der stadium eine thunderbolt crashed makeando van todo die bovino public eine somptuoso barbecue. Gebaked meatballs und grilled sausages was todo around volantes und presto die internazionale Rubicond Kreutz parachuted aan die englandos liberados ketchup saus, bier und french fries por complete der party.

"Aber esse full van BSE!" objected Psychodramma perplexe.

"If digest Christmas pudding, die engelandos can todo digest!" reassured Cabillot.

Cabillot und Psychodramma, mit muchissimo merry celebrated als echte heroes, after dansantes und trinkantes de fulle nacht, zum primero morningo coudde tenfinally from London departe. In de Dover harbour ellos was embarqued op de Britannia, conducted by de Queen Elisabetha personally und returned gloriosamente op der continent. Zuback in Brussel, Cabillot went seine report aan Capitain What presentante.

"Magnificos complimentos, inspector por der success des mission. Die impostor Margaretta Primera esse eine doppel-decker hamburgeresse become und unsere Queen tenfinally Buckingham Palace habe recovered. You habe Europa saved van die bovino invader!" so declared bombasticamente Capitan What.

"Bedankes Capitain. Aber Ich want eine pregunta toi make. Porqué missed zweimal de target? Probabile, tu knewde dat Psychodramma was noch in der stadium bloqued und wachted que ella secure escaped out des stadium?" inquired Cabillot curioso.

"Ich knewde nada at all. Nor missed Ich keine target, liebe inspector! Mit de first zwei rokettes Ich destroyed de MI5 headquartier! You know, es was mucho tempo dat Ich wanted alcunos old counts settle mit meine antiqua paterland!"

5

Cabillot und der Tripoli pizza surprise

Der zommer explodente, Cabillot was aan seine holidags thinkante. Ensemble mit Psychodramma, ello decided de go eine pair weeks spende op de italianse marino resort des Porto Garibaldi.

"Garibaldi? Ich thinked dat esse eine aperitivo! Amusante que ter contre esse eine playa!" exclamed de cyclopa seine neue bermudas exibente.

"Esse keine aperitivo, esse eine caffee brand!" corrected Cabillot die was eine intellectuale hombre.

"Toi gusta meine multicolor bermuda?" inquired Psychodramma mucho coquettely. Cabillot raised die eyos des geomappa und regarded.

"Exilarantes! Aber reminde moi something... Donde verkauffed?" inquired mumblante.

"In front des Europeano Parlamiento..." responded evasively de cyclopa.

"Ah! No tell moi dat you collected die europeanos country bandieras por make teine bermudas. Aber dat esse mucho correcto nicht!" objected der inspector.

"Porqué? De starred union bandiera touched Ich nicht! Esse de only left!" justified de cyclopa mucho patriotically.

Por seine trip nach Italia Cabillot hadde eine autocarro campertrailer rent, so dat van bastante room de cyclopa disposed. Aber, mit feminas travellantes, room esse never bastante. Diese augusto morningo, in der courtyardo des Europeane Polizei buildingo, der inspector was die vehiclo controlante und die cyclopicos baggages attemptante inside des autocarro te stuffe.

"Can Ich de fishing net take?" pregunted Psychodramma.

"OK, aber uno basta!"

"Und die tennis raquettes?"

"Take well!"

"Ohne meine accordeone can Ich survive nicht!"

"If esse por survival, how can Ich impeachemento make!"

"Und meine petanque bowls?"

"Take tambien!"

"Meine depilazion crema...?"

"Psycho, Ich habe nada contra toi teine legs depilante. Aber zwei barrels van zitrone depilazion crema esse tropo much!" objected Cabillot.

"No can sunbronze als eine gorilla hairyose!" protested de cyclopa.

"Unterstuddo! Charge teine depilazion crema op board!" sich resigned der inspector.

"Esse bastante platz por meine windsurfo?" noch addizionned Psychodramma.

"Ah, no! Dat esse tropo grosse! Donde stuffe?"

"Can fixe aan der top des trailer!"

"OK! Necessite anders?"

"Meine enflatable canotto!"

"Take if really want. Aber youself enflate diese sort van Zeppellin dirigible!"

"Necessite tambien meine parasol!" insisted de novo Psychodramma. Dann Cabillot de pazience loste:

"Listen, amiga! Teine parasol esse as grande as die Bouglione Circus tent! No esse platz op meine autocarro!"

Despite des many discussions, op diese postmeridio Cabillot und Psychodramma allegramente managed te departe from Brussel nach der Sud dirigentes. De cyclopa hadde winned: seine parasol was op der autocarro geloaded.

De travel Europa ohne borders traversante was mucho pleasante. Partodo man coudde in Euro bezale. Ten last, in eine luminose morning, die zwei collegas by Porto Garibaldi arrived und op der sea playa sich camped. Die gigantische parasol mit eine cyclopa under der sonne bronzante subito attracted de curiosity des indigenos who thinked dat echte der Bouglione Circus hadde arrived. Moltos bambinos allegros runnantes sich amassed by der sea bord, mit seine fishing cane Psychodramma annoyantes und mucho clamor makeantes. Cabillot uslessy attempted de ellos chase aweg, plastica bottles und empty sardinas box versus ellos projectante. Aber was necessario nicht. Porqué quando seine mammas die belgische car-plates remarqued op el campertrailer, mucho unquietas subito seine bambinos zuback recalled.

"Escape presto! Dat esse eine convoy pedophile belgishe priests!" screamed die mammas. Und alles bambinos evaporated in eine instant.

"Ah! Tenfinally! Wat pax, wat silente marine panorama!" exclamed Cabillot relaxante terwhile dat Psychodramma was alnoch sleepingante. Der primero holidag passed so tranquilo. Zum der sonne sunsettante, Psychodramma sich wakened van seine monolitica siesta.

"Habe etwas appetite! Wat wir masticantes?" inquired de cyclopa op der sand stirringante.

"Must esse eine chinese take-via someplatz!" dixit Cabillot der horizon scannerante.

"No necessite! Make fish barbecue!" objected Psychodramma.

"Aber donde esse der fish?" pregunted Cabillot skeptico.

"Voila!" dixit de cyclopa der net in der sea throwante und eine miraculoso catch performante van manige hitticos exemplaros.

Die zwei polizeros eine gigantische barbecue op der sea playa prepared. Presto der perfume des grilled pescado so strong sich diffused dat slowemente die bambinos zuruck returned, esta time tambien mit seine mammas und papas, und grossemammas und grossepapas, und seine cattos die moustachos thrillantes. Ellos permaned silentemente regardantes die rubicondes flames in der dark dansantes und der savouroso pescado fumigante. Psychodramma cordialmente los invited zum dinner. Aan debutto hesitantes, quando die cyclopa seine windsurfo als eine dinner table arranged, todos sich comfortable maked. Sommige cultivatores proxime inhabitantes, mit eine autotank van vino full arrived op der sea plage und fiestantes der gruppo joined. Everytodos masticated und trinked mucho jubilantes under der lunare lux. Pscyhodramma dann embraced seine accordeone, romantica canzonas tunante und passionnately cantante. Nomanno van die indigenos auscultantes never expected dat eine cycolpa so mucho sociable coudde esse. Aan der end des soirée todos maked muchos complimentos und warme rethankantes, contentissimos und drunkissimos, home returned.

Cabillot und Psychodramma retired under de circus tent mucho fatigued und by der vino obnubilados, alnoch pregustantes eine salutaire sleep. Aber in der profundo des nacht eine horrido whizze noisemente raised und die tent encircled. Alarmed, Cabillot pointed seine lamp in der dark: eine menaceante tornado van insectos was in der air whirlpoolante, als de mamma van alles de jacuzzi gurglante. Es was die terribles padanos mosquitos, qui hadde der odour des humane blood smelled und was maintenow op der point van attack!

"Psycho!" shouted Cabillot clamante, "urgente bringe bitte teine zitrone depilazion crema!"

Die depilazion barrels openingantes, die zwei vacanzeros rapido sich overspreadde van crema exacto in tempo por der attack to prevent. Die mosquitos roketted contra seine target in de crema stikkantes und miserablemente suffocantes. Durante der fulle nacht die mosquitos permaned flyantes over de circus tent als indianos op der bellicose path, seine fort-apache ferox expectantes. Aber mit der helpo des crema die zwei vacanzeros salvaged seine skin. In der morningale sonne radiante, die mosquitos sich retreated mucho humidos und chilled, seine fatigued wings wettamente flappantes. Aber before de abandon der battling campo, der most grosse mosquito chief 'Syringo drillante' solemne dixit: "No finish aquì! Hombre pallido, teine skin shal Ich sanguinario picke!"

Diese brillante dag Cabillot und Psychodramma in der sea swimmantes, op der playa ballone playantes, in der meridio eine long siesta savourante, mucho amused und der nervoso system decompressed. In de most calientes horas, ellos sich refuged under die tent, cards playantes mit locales fishermannos. Op eveningos was siempre eine permanente fiesta mit musica und dance. Aber eine mucho windy postmeridio, terwhile dat Cabillot was crossverba solvente, eine travelante pigeon op der thirtyquatro vertical eine fecale croquette dropped, dann next des inspector landed. Der pigeon hadde eine message mit eine lace round des foot gefixed. Cabillot taked und lectured: "Dumbe und stupidissime inspector! Ter place van teine emergency mobilofono tu habe meine electrico razor emported! Call moi subito! Der razor guarantee esse over und dann some mucho serious happened! Capitain What." Cabillot uberjumped Psychodramma somnolente, nach eine telefoncabin precipitante.

"Hallococco! Hier Cabillot speakingante!"

"Tenfinally, inspector! Primero, warnung nicht meine razor verbrake mit die sand! Cost eine lot dinero! Secundero, wir necessite you. Some mysteriosos phenomenos esse signalled in Sud Italia."

"Wat phenomenos?"

"Sommige fishermannos affirme de habe detected eine gigantische pizza in der sea op bellavista flottante!"

"Eine pizza... op der sea?"

"Ja. So you must nach Trapani fahren und discreto investigate. Take contacto mit der marshallo Deodoro Intimatico, des italiana polizia."

"Aber eine pizza..."

"Keine hesitatione! Orders esse orders!"

"Yesful, Capitain!"

Cabillot nach de playa zurucked und aan Psychodramma expliqued:

"Wir must eine poquito pizza-hunting practice make..."

Es was eine mucho tristefulle adiòs. Die indigenos, sinceras lachrymas sprayantes, sich grouped op der playa melancholicos tunes cantantes und flowers aan de cyclopa offerentes. Mit de cyclopa und seine amigo, ellos hadde maestosos dags spent und mucho jubilated. Cabillot bethanked mucho alles und once recharged der autocarro, jumped op board. Ello knewde nicht dat inside des refolded circus tent was hidden Syringo Drillante mit toda seine tribe van sanguinarios mosquitos. Diese late augusto postermido, der inspector und die cyclopa wroummed aweg claxonnantes van die playa donde mucho allegros vacationned.

Op der nexte late morningo, Trapani was in vista. Cabillot parked seine autocarro by der ferry embarcadero. Nomanno was around. Solo eine picturesque officero mit witte uniforme und colorfulle plumaggio op der casque, unter der sonne immobile sentinellante.

"Marshallo Deodoro Intimatico?"

"In persona. Inspector Cabillot, Ich suppose!"

"Moiself! Und voilà meine assistante, Sergeant Psychodramma."

"Enchanted!" repliqued der polizero eine poquito timorous, militaire decorosamente salutante. Dann pregunted:

"You esse greeka?"

"Ja, plus precisamente cyclopica," responded Psychodramma.

"Meine grossepapa was greeko tambien," repliqued der marshallo.

"Ah, from desde?"

"Sporadico"

"Ah! Was lui tambien polizero?"

"No, philosofo"

"Ah! Meine olde boyfriend was philosofo tambien!"

"Aristotelico?"

"No. Platonico. Dat esse porqué lo abandoned..." concluded Psychodramma.

Zum dat point, Cabillot impatiente interrupted die personale conversatione van seine assistantes:

"Marshallo, explique moi bitte wat esse happeningante aquì."

"Rapido dixit! Inspector, follow moi." Der marshallo des embarcadero descended op der playa waar in der shadowose sombra eine ambulancia parqued was. Inside reposante was eine mucho shocked hombre assisted by uno carabiniero.

"Esse eine localo fishermanno. Yesterdag posmeridio was founded out in der sea escapante, mit seine boat op der playa gestranded und als eine hooligano van horrore screamingante.

"Wat passe?" pregunted Cabillot aan der hombre approchante.

"Daar over!" reclamed der fishermanno der alto sea outside indiquante.

"Wat esse daar over?" insisted der inspector. Der desperado hombre, die eyos paralized, was iperbarico gaspante. El hesitante, dann dixit, mit strange quietnesse:

"Eine pizza! Eine gigantische flottingante pizza!" Aber es was de quietnesse des folly und diese sentence declamada, der fishermanno sinked in eine abyssale trance.

"Dat esse wat go repeatingante since yesterdag," precised der marshallo.

Cabillot exit des ambulancia und permaned der horizon investigante: only witte foam out des waves sparklingante, dann der immenso marine blaue der sky glitteringante.

"Lets prospecte eine poquito around. Ich shal mit der fishermanno boat sail und you shal follow moi cautious swimmante," suggested Cabillot aan Psychodramma. Dann aan der polizero dixit:

"Marshallo, you bitte cover meine retreat in case van danger."

Beide adventured nach der alto sea. Circa eine couple horas later, der sonne was alnoch sunsettante, der sea plus und plus shakerante, mit darke waves rollantes. De cyclopa was placida splashante, als eine unoffensivo mobidick, wasser zum de air sprincklante. Sommige hundred metros adelante, Cabillot was circumspecto navigante. Nada, absolute nada in vista. Der inspector was op der point de zuruck returne, quando sudden in front des boat appeared eine gigantische pizza neapolitana flottante. Was grande als eine fuss-balle campus, mit scarce mozzarella aber mucho tomato. Oregano was bastante, anchovies in abundanza und der perfumo appetissante.

"Psycho! Pizza ahead!" clamed Cabillot. De cyclopa was astonished approximante quando from der alto sky eine robuste noise invisible condensed, dann eine monstruosa multitude van mosquitos die zwei polizeros fulminated, furiosamente pickante. Was Syringo Drillante und seine cannibale tribe op vendetta gekomen. Presto Psychodramma submerged under der sea. Cabillot in seine boat navigante, por reflexion hadde tempo nicht. Improvisto jumped over de pizza, sichself in die melted mozzarella hidingante als protectivo shield. Syringo coudde nicht eine andere hittende sturm performe mit seine patrol contra die gluante mozzarella und retreated op alto por seine batallions reorganize. Psychodramma dann emerged, ohne air pantingante und ella tambien under de mozzarella shelterante.

"Psycho!" called Cabillot, "shoot der distress signal aan der marshallo!"

"Wat esse der distress signal?" pregunted confused la cyclopa.

"Anywat you want! Invente!" implored der inspector.

Dann de greeka cyclopa mit eine handful tomato und mozzarella eine bomba impasted und throwde nach der coast.

Der marshallo op el embarcadero expectante was preciso hit und down gesmashed in eine gluante, aromatico pomodoroso mix.

"Por thousand mounting carabinieros!" exclamde der polizero eine finger suckante, "dat esse pizza, mit anchovies authentica!"

Pointed seine telescopio nach der alto sea, und subito remarqued die zwei naufragantes op de pizza in distress und by eine zwarte cloud van mosquitos attaqued.

"Presto Salvatore! Prepare die Autan Teleshower!" alerted der marshallo. De carabiniero mounted op der summit des ambulancia eine grosse shower gun discoverante und pointingante versus der sea.

"Fire!" ordered der marshallo und subito eine witte jet spritzed out des gun als eine flashante comet over der blaue sea. Improvisto van insectizide sprinkled, die mosquitos dispersed, dolorosamente buzzantes, in der sea kamikazeantes. Syringo Drillante hardemente der massacre escaped, mucho low flyingante. Hateful imprecante, seine anathema proclamed:

"Pallido hombre, no finish aquì! Sooner oder later, Ich shal van transfusion toi kill!"

Op der pizza navigantes, Cabillot und Psychodramma managed by de playa te strande. Mit robustas ropes de pizza was zum embarcadero anchored by industriosos carabinieros. De fulle harbour was circumscripto und verboden accesso.

"Marshallo, wat make if arrive eine andere pizza?" pregunted eine carabiniero.

"Wir commande eine pair biers!" responded brillante der officero.

Presto eine inspection des pizza was ordered. Der Chemicale Brigade des carabinieros op der spot arrived und analyzed die pizza surface.

"Echte buffalesse mozzarella, italianse tomatoes, hispanische anchovies, toscano olive oil und ordinario oregano," was der diagnosis.

De nacht durante, nomanno coudde sleep. Die carabinieros op der playa, der inspector und de cyclopa in seine circus tent camped remained alles tempo de pizza suspiciosos perscrutantes. Aber als in eine enchantamento, presto in der morningo todos falled profundos dormantes. Der sonne was alnoch splendente quando eine carabiniero rewakenante

Diego Marani

shouted van terror:

"De pizza habe desappeared! De pizza esse off!"

Todos jumped out marvellantes. Die ropes was cut, some flaques tomatoes was op die waves noch flottantes.

Por de fulle dag die carabinieros inspected der coast und der sea zum der quest des pizza. No signo, no track, no indicatio was founded. Ter fall des nacht, de same carabiniero aan de marshallo pregunted:

"Marshallo, wat make ahora?"

"Hope dat eine andere come. Diese time prefero eine Capricciosa!" responded noch mucho brillante der offizero.

Effectivamente, de morningo followante, eine andere pizza by de playa was driftingante. Aber noch eine neapolitana. Ex novo, die carabinieros aan der embarcadero de pizza anchored und again permaned alles nacht vigilantes. Aber again by der morningo todos dormantes falled und de pizza secretamente desappeared ter while que later eine andere arrived, altime neapolitana. Es was eine pizza exodus.

"Dat make moi thinke aan somewat mithological..." observed Psychodramma seine face mumblosa scratchante.

"Nexte nacht Ich shal op eine boat offshore permane vigilante. Und als Ich abnormale phenomenos remarque, Ich shal you todos rewake teine accordeone playante," proposed mucho intelligente Cabillot.

"Dann play bitte eine tango. Ich palpito por tangos!" demanded romantica Psychodramma, die after todo noch eine dama was.

De nacht was stille und mucho starfulle. Aber was keine luna visible. In seine boat spyante, Cabillot was alerto wachtante. Nada happened tot der primero morningo. Dann, improvisto out des pizza sprinkled subtiles jets van gas die everymanno made dormantes. Everymanno, excepto Cabillot. Dann, in der swashing des placido sea, die pizza als eine casserole lid

71

opened und from inside exit eine multitudo hombres silentes.

"Clandestinos migrantes!" exclamed Cabillot astonishante, dann rapido embraced de accordeone und eine voluptuoso argentino tango der morningale silence broked.

Aan der sound van der "Tango des Capineras", todos die clandestinos migrantes was capturados by die carabinieros.

"Ich knewde dat must esse somewat mithological!" dixit Psychodramma exultante.

"Correcto! Als die Troy Horsecheval! Die clandestinos under des crusta des pizza hidde, in der nacht der somnifero gas released, dann evaded und sich dispersed around! Dann die ferrymanno mit de pizzaferry zubacked nach Lybia por eine andere chargemento make!" guessed der marshallo illuminato.

"Und ahora, wat shal you make van die clandestinos?" inquired de cyclopa premurosa.

"Ellos shal der permit habe eine megapizza bar open offshore des Trapani harbour por turistas mit boats transitante!" reassured der marshallo mucho sympathetico.

In der meantempo, Cabillot was der boss des gang interrogeante:

"Wat name?"

"Oxo Madoxo, ferrymanno mit poco scrupules und brazene, culottosa face!"

"You esse under arresto!"

"No finish aquì!" menaced der criminalo terwhile que die carabinieros ello tracted aweg. Aber inspector Cabillot hadde dat alnoch muchas times entended.

Aquello morningo, before de departe, Cabillot eine telefonruf to Brussel maked:

"Hallococco, Capitain What? Mission accomplished! De pizza gang esse disfeated!"

"Mucho gut, inspector! Und wat about meine electrico razor?"

"Ah! Dat habe Ich in hostage taken!"

"Eh? Wat signifique?"

"Signifique dat Ich op vacanza premium permane noch eine month. Alterwise teine razor offer Ich aan eine clandestino refugiado!"

"Maledamned Inspector! Unterstuddo! Tu habe eine month vacanza premium winned!"

In Porto Garibaldi returnantes Cabillot und Psychodramma was mucho amicablemente welcomed und die fiestas, die cyclopicos barbecues, die dismoderate dances man noch todag remember op die joyfulle italianische coast.

6

Cabillot und der prodigiose cravate affaire

Was eine only thing van Psychodramma dat Cabillot echte coudde stand nicht: dat aan de ende des jeder sommer, zuback des vakanzas, ella altime fruit confituras por der winter maked. So todo der officio des Europeane Polizei was ful van alles sort van berries, abricots, melons und figos in grosses casseroles boilentes und fermentantes, mucho gluante odour producente, under die boots stickante und manige wasps attrayante.

"Esse tambien por meine muttones! Maintenow esse nomanno op meine islanda who confituras por ellos cooke!" sich justified de cyclopa aan der inspector in eine kant snortante while seine hebdomadario europanto crossverba solvente. Diese postmeridio, de cyclopa was die zitrone confitura in die pots enfermante.

"Where alles stradas directe esse. Quatro litteras..." lectured Cabillot por distractione.

"Eine platz mit quatro litteras? Cuba!" suggested Psychodramma.

"Mmm! Nein, es werke nicht! Wat make van teine classical culture! Ich thinked you esse eine intellectuale!" protested bitteramente der inspector.

"Ich esse van arcadische civilisatione! Insulte nicht, alsyoubitte!"

"Arcadische pastorale toch maxime rurale und ignorante!" insisted der inspector eine quarrel litigioso pursuante. Aber der time de quarrel ellos hadde nicht, porqué subito der telefono dringed.

"Hallococco, Cabillot speakingante!"

"Inspector! Wat esse die odour van burned candies dat from teine fenestra exale? Esse daar bambinos mit der fire playantes?"

"Nein Capitain! Esse Psychodramma winter provisiones preparante!"

"Ah! Dann basta mit passetempos! Come aquì presto! Ich necessito urgente teine advise."

Als usual, Inspector Cabillot taked der liftor und sich presented in der officio des Capitain What alnoch resigned por eine andere mission departe.

"Wat happen diese time? Terroristos die want Euros in zwarte beans transforme?" pregunted ironico der inspector an Capitain What eine geomappa consultante.

"No, mucho worse! Yesterdag wir habe eine telefonruf received des marshallo Deodoro Intimatico, vanout Trapani. Der terrible Oxo Madoxo sich evaded des prison. Und justo todag, diese letter was in de postbox." Capitain What handed eine paper aan Cabillot:

VENDETTA, TREMENDA VENDETTA!
WIR SHAL HERR DRAGHI CRAVATE CUT
MORTE AAN EUROPA!

Oxo Madoxo
Finnko Brutaalo
Frictos Kalamaros
Dr. Guzman

"Habe remarqued die signaturas?" demanded Capitain What.

"Ich habe. Die most dangerosos europeanos criminalos united contra Europa combatantes! Aber who cares des cravate de Herr Draghi? Habe bastante money por buy eine andere!"

"Stupidissimo inspector! Know nicht dat de fuerza des Euro esse in Herr Draghi cravate?"

"Realmente? Als Sansone hair?"

"Exacto! Herr Draghi cravate esse prodigiose! If someuno cut Herr Draghi cravate, de Euro shal falle in todos die markets und Europa shal banquerupte! Antes, nomanno knewde der secret. Aber maintenow, wat shal happen if die Americanos und die Chinesos know!"

"Basta enferme Herr Draghi in seine bank und voilà esse keine risk plus!"

"Nein! Dat esse so facile nicht! Herr Draghi departe morgen por seine holidag!"

"Holidag? Waar go?"

"Eurodisney!"

"Eurodisney? Strange distractio por eine bankiero!" remarqued Cabillot.

"Wat strange? Banquieros endure mucho stress und necessite mucho simple distractios!" expliqued Capitain What.

"Dann, porqué nicht reporte die holidag?" pregunted der inspector.

"Maintenow esse impossibile de reporte, alterwhise die markets percepte dat somewat abnormal esse happenante. Herr Draghi must in Eurodisney gehen und tranquilo sich amuse ! Por der sake des Euro, you shal seine cravate protecte, inspector!"

"Ah! Merdenvolle mundo!" imprecated Cabillot.

"Inspector, Ich tolerate diese vocabulary nicht!"

"Perdone Capitain. Zum teine orders! Hasta Europa siempre!" sich corrected der inspector eine presentarms performante.

"Hasta!" responded der Capitain der martiale saluto exchangeante.

Zuback in seine officio, Cabillot dixit aan de cyclopa:

"Psychodramma, close der gas und gehemos aweg. Eine mucho delicate mission nos expecte."

"Aber die confituras esse pronto nicht!"

"No care nada. Wir must Herr Draghi op holidag discretamente followe und seine cravate protecte!"

"Herr Draghi? Der Euro hombre? Who care por seine cravate? Can in der warderobe let?"

"Psychodramma, eine banquiero cannot seine cravate abandone! Als eine capitain seine boat!" responded pronto Cabillot.

Als siempre, antes des departe, die zwei polizeros descended in der laboratorio des Mr. Genius por de speziale equipment collecte.

"Desolated, inspector, aber teine mission so idiotissima esse dat Ich habe echtemente keine speziale equipment. Only can provide eine disguisamento van Mickey Mouse por toi und eine van Dumbo por teine collega! Habe tambien eine pot chili peppers, und eine bottle antipelliculaire hair lotion. Justo in case..." sich excused Mr. Genius.

"Never minde, Mr. Genius! Emballe alsyoubitte, Ich take todo!" dixit Cabillot mucho sure van sichself.

Noch again, keine Eurodisney hotello accepted eine cyclopa accompanied by eine polizero und der maxime promiscuouse duetto hadde to finde eine andere accomodatione. De beste soluzion was de sich disguise directamente in Mickey Mouse und Dumbo und de gehen heberge in die castello des Belle Sleepingante. Diese dolcissima nacht des ende sommer, Psychodramma de luna mirante out des fenestra des castello, sich scratched der longo, elefantiaco nose und thinked dat was eine poquito tropo much, even por eine cyclopa. Aber Cabillot entended seine protest nicht, porqué ello siempre was sleepingante mit tampones in die auriclones.

Presto op morningo, Herr Draghi arrived mit seine gorillas. Por seine holidag, ello hadde dressed eine striped maillot und eine rosso beret, aber siempre seine powerfulle magicale cravate op neck. Mucho desirante de sich precipite in der attractions parque, Herr Draghi wanted beginne mit eine trip over des Seven Dwarfos kleine treno. Solicitamente, seine gorillas maked platz take op eine wagon und sitted next van ello.

"Regarde! Esse tambien Mickey Mouse!" dixit Herr Draghi scherzoso remarquante Cabillot in disguisamento terwhile dat der inspector rapido hadde jumped in der wagon. Mucho emotionned, der prestigioso bankiero demanded der autographo aan der false Mickey Mouse Die gorillas palpated suspiciosos seine revolvers under de chemise, aber concluded dat was part des disguise. Allegro sifflante, der treno departed ter while que die dwarfos were seine tune singantes:

"Ohi! frappe, frappe, frappe smashe bien toda de rocke, ohi frappe, frappe, frappe make presto charcol sorte. Des noise dat makemos nos importe not, porqué mit grosse noise better travalle nos. Et voilà in der fracas alles singe mucho plus! Ohi! frappe, frappe, frappe..."

After alcunos rounds, der treno in eine darke foresta entred, waar die malvagia sorceresse van Wittesnow was ambushante. Aber in veritas de sorceresse was nicht de echte one. Es was Finnko Brutaalo in disguisamento! Der criminalo was seine razor accurato sharpenante und perfido grinnante. Improvisto,

Cabillot remarqued eine sparklante eclaire in der dark und so jumped on Herr Draghi zum protecte. Eine starke und fierce combat followed, mit hurlos, imprecatios und maxime clamor. Nomanno coudde see wat was happeningante. Aan der exit des foresta, die bambinos fiestantes assisted ann der macabro defilé van tres dwarfos scalpados, zwei desrufflados und eine geshaved gorilla. Herr Draghi, ohne plus beret, aber der cravate intacte, was smileando ignorante und contento. Cabillot suspirante was soulaged. Eine ambulance sirenante arrived zum secourso des gescalped dwarfos ter while que die mammas horrificadas die eyos covered aan seine bambinos.

"Salute Mickey Mouse!" dixit der bankario de hand waveante. Dann seine gorillas ello tractent presto aweg. Psychodramma rapido arrived, die auriclones flappante und in seine nose mit die piedones stumblante.

"Wat passed?" pregunted mucho worried.

"Fortunately nada! Aber wir risqued mucho!" responded Cabillot pantingante.

"Tu permane vigilante. Ich follow prudente!" proposed de cyclopa in die crowdosa avenue disappearante.

In der meantempo, Herr Draghi was nach der castello des Belle Sleepingante gehente.

"Ah, Ich want van der summit des towers der panorama admire!" insisted der bankario mit die gorillas perplexos. Reticentes, ello accompagned. After mucho climbing, ello popped enfinally der kopf out des fenestra, lontano prospectante.

"Regarde, Peter Pan volante!" dixit Herr Draghi der sky indiquante. Aber Peter Pan was nicht. Es was Oxo Madoxo in disguisamento who mit eine rope op der roof des castello gefixed, nach Herr Draghi menaceante descended. Subito eine grosse pair scissors des pocket sorted und sich lanced contra der bankario, seine floreale cravate targettante. Aber

Psychodramma vigilante, from der lake des garden eine noseful van aqua pumped und sprayed over Oxo Madoxo.

"Regarde! Dumbo mit Peter Pan aan die pompieros playantes!" exclamde Herr Draghi mucho divertissante. Aber die zwei gorillas ello grasped por die piedones und presto ello tractent aweg. In der meantempo, Oxo Madoxo, under die stronge jets van Psychodramma gaspante, op der roof repaired und by de andere kant escaped.

Cabillot aan secourse des cyclopa arrived, van calor und fatigue transpirante.

"Waar esse maintenow Herr Draghi?" pregunted Psychodramma exausta.

"Ich habe visto nach seine hotello gehente!"

So, tenminder por diese dag, der danger was over. Herr Draghi returned in seine hotello stanza por seine quotidianos mathematicale exercises performe und seine mentale fitness preserve. Die zwei polizeros, mucho fatigados, die mass touristos nonchalantes, over der grass sleepantes falled. Psychodramma was seine confituras dreamingante und Cabillot seine crossverba, quando eine Eurodisney guardia ellos rewakened imprecante:

"Ehi! Tu esse nicht por slapen bezaled! Tu must promenade und politemente der public salute!" dixit seine piedones contra die cyclopa kickante. Der inspector und de cyclopa stande mucho shatteringantes van fatigue und wachte dat der guardia sich distracte por rapido in der castello des Belle Sleepingante repaire und daar permane sleepingantes. After alles, die castello was meant por dat.

Der dag followante, Herr Draghi wanted absolutamente mit Dumbo op der air fly. Die gorillas, mucho perplexos, consented. Aber por precaution, put eine Formula 1 helmet op der kopf des bankario und de cravate knotted inside des shirt. Der fligende Dumbo was echtemente amusante und even die gorillas sich relaxed observante Herr Draghi allegro vacazionante.

"Esse eine poquito freakettone, aber esse eine gutte chap!" remarqued eine gorilla.

"Esse de mythical Fligende Dragon!" objected der altro mucho spiritful. Aber exacto op diese momento, eine andere fligende Dumbo sich approached des authentico fliegende Dumbo. Was Frictos Kalamaros op seine Makako bootship disguised in Dumbo! Ello transported op seine dorsal seine servant Pedro, armed mit eine electrico razor! Die astonished gorillas permaned de mouth blobbantes van stupor. Aber noch anders was arrivante: Psychodramma in elefantico disguise drivingante eine Canadair! Op seine dorsal chevalquante, was Cabillot in Mickey Mouse disguise. Eine aeronavale battle beginned. Die bambinos van todos kants des parque regrupped enthusiasticos clamantes van marvel under der elefantico trio planante. Eine habile manoeuvre performante, Frictos Kalamaros mit der nose van seine Dumbo suctionned der helmet des Herr Draghi aweg. Dann circumvented der adversario und ello assaulted from behind. Pedro was alnoch seine razor contra Herr Draghi cravate brandishente quando mit eine cabrante maelstrommico push, de fligende cyclopa mit der Canadair improvisto der weg aan de Makako crossed, robusto ello knockante. Cabillot op die carlinguante cockpit stande, pronto sprayed in die eyos des Pedro de antipelliculare hair lotion. Der perfido servant screamante subito left der razor und mit die hands sich covered beide eyos nicht plus voyeurantes. Because des knock, de Makako was terriblemente rollante. Frictos Kalamaros coudde seine bootship gouverne nicht plus und precipited splashando in der lake mit eine pirotecnico applause des spectatores exultantes por so eine originalo aerostunting spectacle. De Eurodisney Manageante Directore, who from seine buro hadde der aerostunt assisted, subito prepared eine contract por die Dumbo trio show, aber quando arrived op platz, es was nomanno left. Frictos Kalamaros und seine servant Pedro hadde escaped mucho dolorantes. Cabillot und Psychodramma mit der Canadair maked eine emergencia landingo in eine maïs campus. Herr Draghi mit die gorillas zubacked in seine chambera por die quotidianos mathematicale exercise.

"Porqué die andere can tranquilos vacanze und Ich must alles tempo mathematicale exercise make?" protested der bankario.

"Porqué necessite practise durante die holidag. Alterwise, quando zubacke in der banka tu habe todo forgetted!" explained patiente eine gorilla.

"Merdenfulle!" exploded Herr Draghi seine aritmetico manual kickante.

Der gorilla es ramassed und es opened aan der juste pagina.

"Behave correcto alsyoubitte Herr Draghi, und declame bravo teine quotidiano exercise aloud!"

Resigned, Herr Draghi beginned seine annoyoso task:

"2008 euros minus 2002 euros = 6 euros; 1 euro plus 1 euro = 0 deutschemarcos..."

Luckemente arrived der laste dag des vakanza. Because des stress, Herr Draghi gorillas hadde beina nevrastenicos becomed und sich rewakened horrificados in der nacht, Herr Draghi cravate ripped in thousando pieces dreamingantes.

"Todag Ich want nach der Wilde West Parc!" insisted Herr Draghi die piedones op der soil stampante.

"Unterstuddo! Aber nicht wander tropo aweg!" conceded die gorillas extenuados.

Inderfact, de Wilde West Parc was der most dangeroso platz waar Herr Draghi coudde gehen, porqué daar was ful van rubicondos und plumosos indianos, any facile confondente mit felonicos malfactors.

Cabillot und Psychodramma was alertos in eine vaporoso treno wagon expectantes.

"Ich want aan die diligenza assault spelen!" exclamde Herr Draghi todo excited und jumped op die diligenza proximo departante. In der meantempo dat der diligenza was pulverosa op die pista rocambolante, eine gruppe indianos chevalquantes sich lanced aan seine pursuit hululantes. Cabillot mit seine binocular was attentivo scannante todos die indianos, quando ello hadde eine freezante tremble:

"Psycho! Der ultimo indiano mit die purpurale plumas! Esse Doctor Guzman, de chocodiktator des Petite Guyane Luxemburgeoise!"

Inderfact, eine alieno indiano hadde der pursuivante gruppe joined. Ter place des plastic axe, ello holde in seine hand eine metallico razor por die muttones wool te cutte. Instantaneo, de cyclopa put die vaporosa locomotiva zum maximo turnante und sich catapulted puffante versus die indianos. Guzman rapido hadde op die diligenza jumped. By der fenestra entrante, der criminalo was Herr Draghi por der neck stricto graspante und der razor already op der cravate posingante, quando die locomotiva next des diligenza managed de accoste. Cabillot pronto pulverized die chili peppers over der criminalo who subito sneezante und irritato starnutante, let seine grip van der most precioso neck des Europa und out des vehiclo carambolled. Noch eine time, Herr Draghi cravate was intacto und der value des euro preserved.

"Tu habe meine life salvaged! Ich shal aan alles meine amigos raconte dat Mickey Mouse salvaged meine life!" exclamde Herr Draghi out des diligenza descendente und die hand aan Cabillot shakerante.

Diese postmeridio, die gorillas renclosed Herr Draghi in seine chambera, mit die excusa dat ello hadde seine exercises nicht correcto solved und ten last, der followante morningo, die renommed bankario Frankoforte zubacked. Die gorillas salutantes der cuirassed avioplano der bankario transportante, suspired van relievo.

"Maintenow esse unsere collegas die shal caretake van ello!" exclamed eine gorilla.

Cabillot und de cyclopa were seine costumes refoldantes und seine baggage collectante, quando arrived runnante de Eurodisney Manageante Directore alcunas paginas hilarico showante.

"Meine segnores! Beste complimentos! Hier esse teine contracto! You esse enroled por teine exilarante aviostunt show!" dixit der hombre mucho satisfacto.

"Nein, nein, Herr Directore. Dat interesse nos nicht!" responded Cabillot der kopf shakerante.

"Tu want der double dinero? Voilà der double!" relanced der Directore die numeros op der contracto corrigente.

"Nein, nein! No esse eine question van prize!" objected der inspector in eine telefonbox entrante por Capitain What informe del result des mission.

"Hallococco, Capitain What? Cabillot speakingante! Mission accomplida! De Euro esse salvo und teine pension tambien!"

"Complimentos Cabillot! Ich was secure que you succeded! Aber, wat esse diese noise?" pregunted der Capitan entendente die Manageante Directore op der glas des telefonbox frappante und implorante.

"Oh, nada! Esse der Eurodisney Directore qui want nos

enrole por eine avionico show por der fulle season!" explained Cabillot.

"Dann you must accepte Cabillot! Alterwise die markets coudde some abnormale movimentos suspecte und make der Euro falle!" dixit Capitain What.

"Aber, what habe dat zum make mit eine avionico show, Capitain?"

"Keine objection inspector! Est por der sake des Euro!"

"Ich proteste, Capitain! Ich esse polizero, keine showmanno!" insisted der inspector.

"Cabillot! You must der contracto accepte und der profit caritativo girobanque aan de Europeane Polizei!" ordered Capitain What der telefon hangante.

Des telefonbox sortingante, under die eyos allucinados des cyclopa, Cabillot signed der contracto por der avionico stunt show.

"Dispacke der baggage, Psycho! Wir permane aquì!" dixit der inspector aan seine collega.

Manige weeks later, in Brussel zubackantes, Psychodramma returned aan seine confituras und Cabillot aan seine crossverba, siempre annoyado por diese gluante toch stinkingante confusion in seine officio.

"Psycho, after alles, Ich habe toi in de Europeane Polizei enroled por moi helpe in corssverba solvente, not por confituras make! So, alstubitte, helpe. Where alles stradas directe esse... Wat platz esse?"

"Rome, inspector, Rome!" responded de cyclopa paziente.

"Ah! Dankissimo! Voilà der soluzion! Truefulle! Alles stradas in Rome directe esse! Maintenow es klopte!" exclamde Cabillot mucho reconfortado mit seine collega.

"Wat thinke? Shoudde wir eine souvenir aan Herr Draghi envoy?" pregunted der inspector aan de cyclopa.

"Dat esse eine gutte idea! Wat about eine pot cherry

confitura?" proposed Psychodramma.

"Porqué not!" approved Cabillot thinkante dat so eine pot less was in seine officio restante.

In Frankoforte, Herr Draghi received der pot confitura mit hommagios van Cabillot und Psychodramma. Ello subito calculated:

"1 pot confitura = 1 euro 35 cents," und presto der dinero sent aan die europeanos polizeros, porqué man siempre dixit dat eine europeano bankiero absolute incorruptible must esse.

7

Cabillot und der tandoori nucleare complot

Was der einde des poliziesco achademico jahro und noch eine time Cabillot wanted attempte de passe die competitio por tenfinally Capitain become. Ello supported nicht plus aan die orders des Capitain What permane. Op esto purpose, ello necessited de undegehen eine Proficiente Europantico Crossverba test demonstrante dat seine poliziesco cervelle bastante sofisticated was. Aber Cabillot was mit crossverba mucho smart nicht. Por diese reason, ello disguised in seine cravate eine microfono und put in seine ear eine kopfone mit Psychodramma via telefonmobile in seine officio connected. Confidente der test te passe, der inspector was in de exame salle, pronto por der officiale start des crossverba test. In der mean tempo, ello controlled die radio linkamento mit de cyclopa.

"Pronto, Psycho? Can you ausculte?" dixit whisperante.

"Ausculto, ausculto! Todo esse pronto!" reassured de cyclopa, manige encyclopedias, dizionarios und wikipedios op seine screen openingante.

"Gut! Dann quando Ich pregunto, you responde. Aber prego speake piano, alterwise aquì alles entende!" recommended Cabillot.

De exame salle was eine vitreo hangar die de Europeane Polizei utilized als training platz por seine pompose parade des 9 van Maio. Op eine podium, der Examinante Professor in alta uniforme was die candidatos severissimo scannerante.

"Tu esse aquì por eine honesta competitio make vanout solo die beste shal selectioned esse und become capitanos des gloriosa Europeane Polizei! Augurante you gutte fortune, Ich invite you alles eine honorable und correcto behaviour habe! Que win der best!" dixit der Examinante Professor mit eine grave vox. Presto, op sound van eine trumpette, eine vigoroso officiero op eine witte horse strogoffose chevalquante, mucho solemnemente de exame salle entered, der texto des crossverba in eine sealed enveloppa carringante und in die hands des Professor deponente. Todos die polizeros maked eine elegante presentarms, coralmente proclamed "Hasta Europa siempre!", dann sitted aan seine platz.

Was eine crossverba over generale Europeane culture. Cabillot diligente beginned.

"Esse greca und esse longa, nove litteras!" ello whispered al microfono.

"De Marathona, ignoranto!" responded Psycho.

"Gut! Danke! Noch eine! Franzosa danse: begin mit 'can' und end mit 'can', six litteras!"

"Can-can, ignoranto!"

"Ah! Gut! Eine andere: Finnicos liebe un lot, cinquo litteras!"

"Vodka!"

"Vodka? No fit!"

"Dann try Birra!"

"No fit nochplus!"

"Dann try Gin!"

"Habe trois litteras, nicht cinquo!"

"Ah, dann try Porto!"

"No fit!"

"Dann try Grappa!"

"Habe six litteras!"

"Merdenvolle, wat can esse?" exclamed Psychodramma.

Die internet franticamente googolante, ella remarqued nicht dat Capitain What hadde in seine officio entered und was from der andere kant des desk prospectante.

"Renna! Try renna!" noch suggested exultante la cyclopa.

"No fit nichtplus! Presto, habe poco tempo left!" repliqued Cabillot fremissante. "Sauna! Eureka! Dat esse der solutione!" suddenemente shouted und seine vox resounded echoante in de exame salle from der kopfones. Todos die candidatos sich turned, der platz des inspector regardante. De Examinante Professor stande van seine poltronchair scandalized, de mortificado Cabillot mit lo eyos tempestoso targettante. In Psychodramma officio, Capitain What grasped der microfono und shouted:

"Cabillot forgette der grade van capitain und zubacke subito in teine officio!" De Examinante Professor mucho stiff der porta opened und ohne parolas escorted Cabillot out.

De cyclopa was over die encyclopedia embarrassada skippante quando Cabillot entered seine officio. Capitain What, out des fenestra admirante, turned die shoulders.

"Mucho pity, inspector! Aber you shal eine andere chance habe!" dixit der Capitain falsemente comprensivo. "Maintenow habe wir eine most urgentissima emergenza to face. Und noch again Europa necessite teine helpo!"

"Noch eine annoyamento, you mean?" dixit sarchastico Cabillot.

"Noch eine delicatissima mission, inspector! Diese time you must Europa protect van de indianica folie!"

"Wat esse? Eine neue type van flu?"

"No, eine nucleare bomba! Wir must de nucleare guerra intra India und Pakistan prevent! So you must in India gehen und die nucleare indianica bomba annihilante disconnecte!"

"Esse you jokerante, capitan?"

"No. You esse der unique hombre qui can questa mission performe!"

"Porqué?" demanded flattado Cabillot.

"Porqué Ich habe toi caught cheatingante in eine Proficiente Europantico Crossverba und so Ich can toi blackmaile forever!" explained Capitain What addizionante: "Ah! Und forget nicht unsere agent in loco de contacte!"

"Wie esse?" pregunted Cabillot perplexo.

"De locale promotor des 'Jeux sans frontieres' in India. Hier esse seine telefonumero. Demande van Frau Bhella Gita!" noch dixit der Capitain out del officio sortente.

"India, cinquo litteras. Ex britannische colonia, unione plurietnica van states des subcontinente indianico..." lexit ironica Psychodramma in der wikipedia. Aber Cabillot die ironie appreciated nicht.

"Better chez Mr. Genius gehen!" suggested dann die cyclopa.

Als usual, die zwei polizeros descended in der laboratorio des Mr. Genius, some speziale equipatura demandantes por seine mission.

"Por India? Ah, India! Lets regarde... In India esse ful van Indianos, so can efficace esse eine indiano und eine cow-boy disguisamiento!" dixit Mr. Genius seine catalogo van secretos weapones consultante und eine plumoso hat proposante.

"Echtemente, esto typo van indianos esse in America, not in India Mr. Genius!" objected Psychodramma qui hadde de encyclopedia estudied.

"Ah! Hadde forgetted! Dann if Indianos esse in America, in India must esse ful van Americanos!" concluded arguingante der reserchero.

"No, no! Aquellos esse..." attempted de proteste Psychodramma. Aber Mr. Genius interrupted.

"Keine objectio! Esse moi Mr. Genius oder nicht? So, eine poquito van respect por die science, bitte! Tu Cabillot shal americano esse! Un toi Psychodramma shal Native Indiano. Voilà eine indiano plumoso hat mit plastic axe plus eine kit colorato maquillage und eine pair cow-boy pantalons mit toy pistolas in der belt. Als you both muchissimo sympatico esse, Ich offer tambien eine telefonbook mit yellow paginas und zwei limonades!"

"Zwei limonades?" pregunted Cabillot perplexo.

"Esse todo was ist left, inspector! Wir habe reductiones des budget. Aber remembra de return die limonades botellas! Capitain What esse mucho insistente por economies aquì make!"

Muchissimo deceived, der inspector und die cyclopa paqued seine equippamento in der liftor remontantes.

In der Nova Delhi avioporto man habe habitus de rencounter alles typos van strange, mucho folklorico people. Aber eine myopa und plumosa cyclopa mit uno gringo, nomanno hadde never visto. Aan Cabillot eine truxi[1] expectante, manige hindus marvellantes eine oder zwei pieces van dinero dropped, maybe thinquantes dat der inspector eine domator van wilde beastias was.

"Esse eine abominable himalayano chicken?" alcunos pregunted curiosos.

---

1 Truxi : mix inter eine truck und eine taxi. Est eine grosse, cyclopico taxi.

In India nichtplus, keine hotello accepted eine cyclopa disguised in chicken escorted by eine polizero disguised in gringo. Dat was zu much even for Indianos. Noch again die zwei amigos necessited eine fortunosa accomodation te finde. Eine longa discussion explodes.

"Tu want echetemente que do that?" demanded Cabillot.

"Porqué not?" insisted Psychodramma.

"Porqué por eine polizero esse humiliante soccorso demande aan 'Jeux sans frontieres'! Esse nicht 'Médecins sans frontières'!" protested velenoso Cabillot.

Was tarde nacht quando der telefon dringed in de centrale indianico siege van 'Jeux sans frontieres'.

"Hallo yogo? Ki shnamurti?" eine feminale vox enquired

"Ehm! Hare krishna! Speake europanto, alstubitte?" pregunted Cabillot.

"Suremente! Alles in India speak Europanto! Qui esse telefonrufante?"

"Inspector Cabillot, van de Europeane Polizei. Mr. Genius moi send. Ich esse in speziale mission mit meine collega Psychodramma. Can you bitte nos hospitare por esta nacht?"

"Aber sincerely festose, inspector! Ich esse Bhella Gita, de Mahrajesse van Puttanhore und esse por moi eine honour de you hospitare!" exulted die dama gentile interloquente.

El palace van de Mahrajesse was trulemente eine fabouloso place, mit fountains und gardens, mit witte elefantos de belly dance performantes und naked ballerinas floridos baldaquinos transportantes, mit timidos eunuquos into enflammados rings jumpantes und Bengala tigers die thermale bains preparantes. Zwei guardias escorted los polizeros by der patrona die was seine hosts expectante in der salone des honor.

"Meine modeste bicoque esse aan teine disposal, inspector!"

Diego Marani

dixit de Mahrajesse mit hospitale solicitudo und die hand offered zum kisso van Cabillot. De Mahrajesse van Puttanhore was inderfacts eine charmantissima donna, mit blakke eyos und longo hair. Seine skin was als witte als de sand van eine tropicale playa, van rose und oleosos perfumes scentente. Ella sitted in eine longo canapé, eine tasse van tea mollemente sippante. By eine kant, eine nigro eunuquo mit longo, blondo hair played languido eine lyra. Eine andere eunuquo arrived some drinkes in crystal cups carringante und servente, mucho effeminated der minuscolo bump waverante.

"Prego trinque eine desalterante beveraggio, meine honorable hosts!" invited de dama.

"Danke mucho Mahrajesse. Tu esse maxime hospital. Ohne teine helpo, wir woudde maintenow long der strada mendicantes op caca van vaqua trampelantes!" rethanked Cabillot.

"Meine plaisir, inspector! Aber wat interessantes costumes you dresse!" remarked de Mahrajesse por der primera time seine hosts observante.

"Ah! Dat esse eine idea van nostro Mr. Genius!" sich justified Cabillot rubicondante.

"Tu resemble John Wayne und teine cyclopica collega eine Christmas turquese chicken!" plaisanted die indiana dama. Aber Psychodramma appreciated nicht und maked eine snortante grimace. After der soulageante drinke, die zwei polizeros mucho fatigados, demanded de sich retire por slapen.

"Fuco, accompagne meine hosts in seine apartamentos!" ordonned die dama aan seine eunuquo. Subito der eunuquo die lyra abandonned und escorted lodies zwei amigos op der primero floor, in eine grande sala mit balconnade in der subjacente garden prospiciente.

"Bona nacht!" dixit Fuco de porta closingant. Op die momento, Cabillot perceived eine strange lux in seine eyos.

95

Aquella nacht Cabillot hadde eine troubled sleep und quando sich rewakened felt eine strong pain op der kopf. Around regardante, noticed dat ello was nicht more in die chambera mit balconnade, aber in eine ronde salle. Tambien der bed waar ello stande was ronde. Next des bed was eine tripod mit eine grosse carafe fulle van eine blauwe liquid. Solide bars van iron bloqued der unique, grande fenestra. Der inspector dann sich turned zum der altro kant und presto eine jump maked screamante: op der bed next was Fuco allonged, todo naked solo eine tarzan tanga dressante. Op eine andere side des salle eine grosse laugh exploded. Bhella Gita sich approached divertissante. Ella was solo eine blakke latex bikini dressante und eine metallico whip agitante.

"Bono morningo, inspector! You habe mucho slaped mit meine powerfulle somnifero!"

"Waar esse Psychodramma? Wat esse aquì?" enquired mucho worried Cabillot.

"Psychodramma esse in marinade mit tandoori porqué esta nacht wir shal eine savoured tandoori cyclopa zum dinner serve! Und aquì tu esse in meine personale sexodrome!"

"Sexodrome? No unterstuddo!"

"Inspector, Ich esse eine mucho sofistiquata dama! Sex esse por moi banale, annoyante und van keine relief. Ich habe meine particulare sexuale caprices por satisfaction. By exemplo, mich gusta eine lot de observe meine Fuco in action!" explained die dama desnoch pantelante van excitatione.

"No esse uno eunuquo?" pregunted timido Cabillot.

"Ah, ah! Fuco esse eine falso eunuquo, in reality eine validissimo macho!" exulted Bhella Gita die tongue over seine lips slappante.

"Sorceresse! Que want van moi!" exclamed Cabillot

furioso.

"Que you contente meine Fuco desire!"

"Jamas! Ich esse beidesexuale nicht!" protested der inspector.

"Poco importe! Fuco, trinque!" ordonned de dama excitada.

El eunuquo dann grasped der carafe und engulped todo der blauwe liquid.

"Wat esse?" enquired timoroso Cabillot.

"Viagra shake! Ich habe noch quatro barrels in meine boudoir!" dixit de indianica dama erotica grinningante.

"Wachte! Esse dangerose sex make mit moi! Ich habe hepatite B, syphilis, gonorrhea, AIDS und stinkingante breath!" declared Cabillot eine extremo salvage pathetico pursuingante.

"Fuco tambien!" dixit de dama ohne compassion "Und quando trinque Viagra, become eine beastia van sex famishante!"

"Eh, eh! Me Tarzan, tu Jane!" dixit Fuco sich approachante.

"Vade retro!" intimated Cabillot.

"Sure! Siempre retro, solo retro!" promised Fuco.

Op der same momento de porta des sexodrome blastante got in manige pieces und der wall tambien. Psychodramma emerged out des crumblante rubbles. Ella was solo seine underpants dressingante, toda rubiconda und drippante van tandoori marinade.

"Psychodramma!" dixit Cabillot festose clamante.

"Esse moi, inspector! Estos indianos me somnifered und wanted me cook als eine chicken! Aber ellos knowde nicht dat Ich altime sleep mit eine eyo only!" shouted de cyclopa mucho rageante, seine unico eyo mit der finger indiquante. Bhella Gita attempted de escape, aber de cyclopa grasped de dama por seine neck und la rolled in der bed covers als eine salami ter while que Cabillot captured Fuco und lo knotted mit seine blondo hair aan die fenestra bars als eine spider in seine web.

"Psychodramma, wat happened?" demanded dann der inspector soulaged de recover seine amiga.

"Die balconnade chambera was eine trap! Durante de nacht der bed sich opened und ich sprofounded in eine deepissimo basin ful van tandoori marinade. Ich was mucho weakened por cause des somnifero, aber was sleepingante nicht. Esto morningo, teine screams perceivente, Ich jumped out des basin manige guardias contra der muro smashante und moi voilà!" explained de cyclopa, dann pregunted:

"Aber wat happened toi? Porqué Fuco esse in Tarzan dressed?" pregunted Psychodramma de eunuquo imprisoned op de fenestra indiquante.

"Nada, nada! Eine dag Ich shal explaine..." responded evasivo Cabillot.

Die zwei prisoneros were rabidosos grinningantes. Der inspector sich approached des dama.

"You esse van 'Jeux sans frontieres' nicht! Qui esse echtemente?" interroged Cabillot.

"Ich esse Bhrutta Putra, eine secreto indiano agente," confessed tenfinally de criminala.

"Und waar esse de echte Bhella Gita?" demanded der inspector.

"In der acide dissolved! Die puttenhore diese end deserved! Porqué ella attempted de sabotage unsere bomba! Und der same shal happen you as presto que meine collegas des secreto service esse alerted!" dixit de false Mahrajesse.

"Assassina! Nomanno shal salvage you! Speake! Waar esse die bomba."

"Maldido Cabillot! Ich shal never tell!" menaced Bhrutta Putra.

Cabillot dann regarded Fuco op des fenestra bars agitato flungante, seine Tarzan tanga mucho montgolfierante. Suddenemente der inspector hadde eine wundermarvellouse idea.

"Speake, oder Ich shal Fuco liberate und mit ello toi enclose!"

"Ah! No, Fuco no! Fuco esse eine animalo!"

"Speake!"

"Gut, maldido inspector! Ich speake! De bomba esse aquì, in meine secreto boudoir, unter der tandoori basin. Aber you can nicht make por stoppe! Alles esse pronto por fire die bomba nach Pakistan! In 30 minutos Islamabad shal nicht more existe!"

"Accompagne nos zum der basin!" ordered Cabillot de dama liberante ter while que Psychodramma out des fenestra de grille mit Fuco noch well knotted distached und aweg tracted.

In de balconnade chambera was inderfacts eine grosso cuirassed liftor die nach eine underground hangar descended. Daar studde eine grosse rocketto desnoch fumigante.

"Esto esse teine boudoir?" pregunted suspectoso Cabillot.

"Ja. Ich liebe de nominate sic!" responded de false Mahrajesse.

Der inspector was around regardante eine strategico plan estudiante.

"Presto, take die nucleare barrels in der liftor und put inside der rocketto diese Viagra shake barrels!" dixit improvisto aan Bhrutta Putra eine stock blauwe barrels indiquante. While speakante, Cabillot remarqued dat op der altro kant des hangar stande noch manige rosso barrels.

"Wat esse die rossos!" pregunted.

"Esse Tandoori marinade," responded la dama.

"Put inside des rocketto tambien!" ordered again der

inspector.

Der chargemento was beina over quando eine grosse flame bursted desde der motor, die muros des hangar trembled und mucho roboante der rocketto was powerfulle in der sky propulsed, eine grosse cloud in der hangar shufflante.

Quando der cloud dissolved, in der nocturno sky was noch visible eine palpitante flame aweg andante. Cabillot dann grasped Bhrutta Putra por eine arm.

"Wat make van moi, cruellissimo polizero! Habe nicht pity van eine unoffensiva dama?" implored die false Mahrajesse.

"No!" responded laconico Cabillot die, quando wanted, coudde eine echte duro macho esse.

"If you want moi kille, dann kille! Ich shal als eine indianica heroesse martyricamente trespasse!" dixit solemne de criminala.

"No, keine kill! Cabillot no kill jamas. Tu shal eine longo travel make..."

"Eine longo travel! Waar exporte moi? In eine Europeane prison?"

"No. Zu much comfortable!" dixit der inspector Bhrutta Putra in der liftor pushante.

"You shal por eine nucleare trip op der cosmo departe! Und mit mucha gustosa company!" noch explained Cabillot sinistro smileante und die eyos luxurioso winkante. Dann aan die cyclopa ordonned:

"Psycho, desknotte Fuco und charge ello tambien in der liftor!"

"Aaagh! No, Fuco no!" cried die false Mahrajesse. Aber ter while que die portas des liftor closed, Cabillot der ultimo flor button pushed. Eine sparkeante burst around petardante bombarded, und noch eine grosse flame vamped unter des liftor qui molto shakerante shuffled aweg in der cosmo mysterioso.

Alcunos minutos after, die viagra mit tandoori rocketto exploded over Islamabad, de volle city van rubro, dann van blauw colorante, als eine toilet detergente. Imprecantes pakistanos, dirty van rubicondo mud, nach derel sky furiosos menaceantes seine hand, presto experienced eine strange sexuale excitatio. In poco time, die stradas van de pakistane capitale becomed eine ambulante sex show. Nomanno coudde sich restrain van sexuale exercises te performe. Die syrenes clamorantes, die ambulances wroummantes, de volle city was in eine totale pandemonio. Subito, die pakistane armada eine adequata retaliazione contra India triggered. Out des mountains des Cachemire, eine rocketto ful van curcuma und chili peppers over New Dehli exploded, de volle city van yellow colorante, alles peoples rumorosos sneezantes, die eyos piquantes und der nose droppante. Psychodramma tambien, die alnoch was tandoori rubra, sich covered van eine yellow paste.

"Presto shutte die fenestras!" urged de cyclopa aan Cabillot vomitoso spittante. Op aquello moment der telefon ruffed.

"Hallococco! Wie speakante?" dixit eine mucho rabidosa voice

"Jeux sans frontieres. Wat desire?" responded professionale der inspector.

"Cabillot! Aquì Capitain What speakante! Wat passe? Nostros radars detecte mucha turbolence in der subcontinente indianico!"

"De indianos esse inderfacts incontinentes, meine Capitan. Aquì infuriate eine spice war!" explained Cabillot.

"Eine spice war? Wat signifique, inspector?" pregunted alarmed der Capitan. Aber presto eine forte whistle seine vox suffoqued, followed by eine rumble tempestoso cannonante.

"Hallococco! Inspector! Wat happen! You noch entende?" inquired shoutante Capitain What.

"Keine worry, Capitan! Was eine witte pepper bomba! Perdone if esse sneezante!" dixit Cabillot seine nose pruriginoso scratchante.

"Inspector, Ich constate que you habe teine mission manifestamente failed! India und Pakistan esse maintenow in eine spice war belligerantes!"

"Better eine spice war dann eine space war, Capitan. After alles, was der best que coudde do mit zwei limonades! Tu noch want die botellas zuback?" enquired ironico Cabillot.

"Inspector! Minde teine vocabulario mit eine superior speakante! Tu esse Capitain nicht!" repliqued screamante der alto officero.

"Perdone Capitain, aber maintenow Ich must der telefon hang und eine refuge finde porqué aquì rain moscade nutmegs! Adios! If no come zuback, trinque eine lemonade in meine memoria!" dixit noch Cabillot der telefon apparato abandonnante, unter eine mitraillade van perfumante moscade nuts runnante und seine kopf mit de yellowpaginas protegente.

8

Cabillot und der Linguistische Resistenza

Was der jahro 2035 quando Europa formalmente become eine province des Chinese imperio und der Europeane Unione eine agency des Chinese governemento. Alles mundo, since mucho tiempo, was diese disvelopment expectante. Europe hadde keine power anyplus: die Europeane industrias was alles gekauffed by Chinos und der Euro was replaced by der Yen. Aber der passage des powers in Bruxel was mucho tense und tumultuose. Protestationes exploded partodo in diese dags und der policia arrested manige manifestantes. Der army was disployed in nevralgicale platzen und publique offices was closed. Op diese autumnale morningo, der president des EU Commissione assisted aan der depositione des blaue Europeane flag which was replaced mit der rode Chinese flag. Der neue Chinese governator was aan seine side und shaked hands mucho malignemente. Maintenow el was der boss des Europa!

Inspector Cabillot tambien was among der commotioned crowd. Aber in disguise. El escaped seine officio por avoid arrestatione. Since alcunos months already Cabillot was in der Resistenza combatante por der liberatione van Europe. Der inspector assisted tranquil aan der ceremony, ausculted der militaire Chinese banda trumpetingante der Europeane anthem, dann walked silentiose aweg in der metro corridors unter des EU headquartieros und desolated disbarqued in eine centrale park. El was orders expectingante from seine comandantes, aber nomanno yet lo contacted. Improviste seine mobilofono ringobelled.

"Hallococco, wie speakante?"
"Cabillot, aquì Captain What!"
"Captain! Ich thinqued dat you was in eine Chinese prison!"

Since quando clandestino becomed, Cabillot never plus hadde noticias van seine superior. Alles Europese manageros was arrested by Chineses und replaced mit Chinos. Solo kleine clerickos was preserved from epuratione.

"Inspector, Ich esse eine olde britishe fox, und know benissimo how to illusion eine Chino! Aquì London, Ich esse todag der comandante des EUBUFRECARSULIBAR Europese Unione Burocratische-Free Carbon-Sustainable Liberatione Army. Ich esse pronto eine message op internet proclame. Ausculte attentive, porqué diese message shal historia become!"

Cabillot suddenemente switched seine internet radio. After eine creakingose scratching, der voice des Captain emerged from der electricale waves:

"Europeanos! Aquì Captain What, Gerald What speakingante! Ich esse der comandante supremo des clandestine Europese Unione Liberatione Army und esse aquì por invite you alles zum Resistenza! Der Chinese impostor habe der control taken van unsere institutiones, van unsere civitates und industrias und militaire barrackas. Mit seine brutale forza, Chinos oblige Europeanos de worke als slaves. Europeanos! Accepte nicht der Chinese chain op teine kopf! Resiste, rebel und revolte! Sabotage mit alles medios der invadente intrusor, unsere advice iedere dag auscultante op radio. Wir shal regulares actiones van sabotage op radio proclame dat you alles must conducte! Zum exemplo, todag wir proclame der European Rice Pissing Day. Go alles piss in rice fields! So dat wir shall pollute Chinese rice und disguste Chinese invaders! Europeanos, wir shal combat ellos in die rice fileds, in die massage parlours, in die lacquered ducks, in die fried noodles, in die souvenir shops, in der launderettes, everydonde ellos hide! Wir shal resurge, powerfulle und liberated from Chinese oppressione!"

Cabillot diswitched der radio und suspired. Captain What never reallemente was eine communicator. Maintenow resembled eine delirante insane. Dat was keine seriouse Resistenza. Dan was Carnaval. Again dringed der mobilofono.

"Inspector! Wat thinke? Was eine impressive message?" pregunted Captain What.

"Impressive toch... Wat esse der nexte? Wat come after der European Rice Pissing Day?"

"Ah, Inspector! Wir habe eine volle series van sabotage actiones planned! Nexte esse der European Fireworks Pissing Day. Wir shal alles pisse op fireworks und so die Chinos shal unable esse de celebrate seine fiestas! Keine firework shal blaste! Mucho depressive por Chinos! Ah, ah, ah!" exclamed der Captain exultante.

Cabillot was skepticale van Captain What methodes. El decided de abandon Resistenza und de acte solitario. El hadde eine better, most diabolische idea.

Algunos dags before, el hadde rent eine kleine shop in front des Europeana Commissione headquartieros. Was eine olde pizza shop, aber Cabillot removed alles furniture, painted blanco, refurbished portales und fenestras, installed tables mit poltronchairs. Dann fixed op top des entrance eine sign: „Speziale English Cursos por Chinos – Moderne Methode – Maxime Resultos".

Pronto eine morningo der primero clilente entered.
    "Hao, hao! Woh whu jong jing gong hao English?"
    "Ja, 50.000.000 yen per hour." Answered Cabillot.
    "Whuao whuao!!!" protested der Chino.
    "Whuao, aber maxime effective," commented der Inspector.
    "Guo gao... Dao juo jio whu," dixit der Chino der wallet openingante.
    "Gut! Dann der curso starte tomorrow zum 8 p.m." explained Cabillot.

Eine monat plus later, Cabillot hadde honderd Chino studentes in seine schola. Alles manageros from Chinese europese officios, alles alto fonctionarios. Ellos believed de esse English learningante. Aber not! Cabillot was Europanto teachingante! Und maxima confusione in seine minds spreadingante...

After algunos tiempos, manige manageros from Cabillot schola was enroled por importante jobs. Und presto nomanno coudde los understande. Eine colossale incomprehensione presto blocked alles Chinese administratione in Europa. Der Chinese governor coudde nicht unterstande wat was happeningante. Alles der Chinese power structura was fallingante. Quarrelose disputes erupted porqué superiores unterstudde nicht inferiores und orders coudde not transmitte. Alles Chinesos in Bruxel speaked perfecte Europanto und believed dat esse English. From Beijingo commandantes unterstudde nicht wat lingua was seine Europese manageros speakante. Rapido, der invasive Chinese machine tilted. Die Chinos lost der control van seine dominatione. Un dag ellos alles embarqued in honderd cargos und swarmed zuback zum China. Slowemente die Europeanos chased alles remainingante invaders away und recovered der power des Europeanes institutiones.

Eine radiose sonne morningo, Capitain What appeared in front des liberated Europeane headquarteros donde again was exposed der blaue Europeane flag. Cabillot tanbien vested eine martiale blaue uniforme mit goldene stars op breast.

In seine officio was desalready Capitain What sittingante op seine poltronchair crossverba composingante.

"Inspector! Als tu can constate, unsere Resistenza was mucho successfulle! Chinos retreated as soon dat wir op rice fields pissed! Was mucho simple de expulse diese invaderos, bedankes aan meine tacticale genius! Voilà mit eine piss die Chinos defeated!" proclamed der Captain makingante eine martiale salute aan der Inspector.

"Sicheremente Captain. Tu was eine heroicale piss combatante!"

Commented der Inspector. In seine officio entered un der portale closed. Immediate der telefon dringed.

"Inspector, Ich esse unable de eine crossverba solve. Wat prevente hombre zum pisse? Acht litteras. Thinked "C-h-i-n-e-s-e" aber worke nicht!" pregunted Capitain What.

"Dan try "p-r-o-s-t-a-t-e" Capitain..." responded Cabillot und der telefono rehanged.

9

De Europanto Bricotouristische Guide

Die vakanzas approchantes, de Hoge Europantico Instituto por Bricotouristik eine rapido curso organize van Europanto conversazie in plurimos leisure argumentos. Mit diese curso, die europantico vakanzeros shal in todo der mundo habiles esse eine essenziale conversazie in Europanto performe und manige novos europanticos encounters make.

I

Conversatio curso por europantouristos: Aan der diskoteka

Vocabulario:

(Eine approximative French-English translatione aquì esse provided por facilitate learning)

Ohé?:   Bonsoir mademoiselle, voudriez vous avoir l'aimabilité de m'accorder une danse? Good evening you elegant lady, would you like to dance with me?

Yesfulle: Certainement. I would be very happy!

Wo pisse?:   Où sont les toilettes, s'il vous plaît?
                              Where are the toilets, please?

Eine pataque: Une belle gonzesse. A beautiful girl.

Eine brustolon: Un pauvre type. An idiot

Vamolà! (colloquial):   Au revoir! Bye, bye!

Puttanesque!:   Salope! Immoral woman!

Heil pataque!:   Salut salope! Hello immoral woman!

Euro und Eura, yonge echte europeanos, encounter make in eine renommed Benidorm discoteka.

Euro: Heil pataque! Ohé?
Eura: No!
Euro: Ah! Dann, Wo pisse?
Eura: Là!

Euro go pisse und zubacke relieved.

Euro: Maybe trink you etwas?
Eura: No!
Euro: Schade! Wat name toi?
Eura: Meine business!
Euro: Wat esse teine supportive bra size?
Eura: Numero 5

Euro:	Ollallà!
Euro:	Esse you espagnola?
Eura:	No!
Euro:	Make moi guesse! You esse portugalla!
Eura:	(mit surprise) How guessed?
Euro:	Because des moustachos!
Eura:	Ah! Dann, you esse groenlandische!
Euro:	(mit surprise) How guessed?
Eura:	Because des hornos over teine kopf!
Euro:	Never der moins, maybe you liebe danse mit moi.
Eura:	Yesfulle! Aber attentio aan meine callous!

Commenzant eine giro vertiginoso. Euro allonge handes tropo much.

Eura:	Wat make? Me palpe op derriero?
Euro:	Ah, excuse. Ich think dat esse teine callous!
Eura:	Porcadillo!
Euro:	Desolated, aber you esse eine pataque und ich puedo resiste nicht!
Eura:	You esse echte eine brustolon!
Euro:	Realmente think? So, porqué danze mit moi?
Eura:	Porqué ich esse Madame Pipì und you habe keine coin op de saucer gedropped!
Euro:	Puttanesque! You habe moi deceived!

Eura pique eine coin out des pokets van Euro, dixit "Vamolà, imbecillo!" und go aweg.

Morale: Never palpe die callous aan unknowne people.

II

Conversatio curso por europantouristos: Aan der seaplaya

Vocabulario:

Mastro natante:	maître nageur / lifeguard
Pedalero:	pédalo
Helpo!:	au secours! / Help!
Recepido:	compris / Understood
Derriero:	derrière / Back

Euro work as mastro natante by eine graciosa mediterranea seaplaya. Todos die dags ello permane by seine pedalero, pronto zum salvage van personas in der water suffocantes. Eura esse eine muchissime beautifulle turistesse, seine tittones onder der sonne bronzante.

Euro: Salve Regina, wat passe?

Eura: (seine parasol lunettas soulevante)
Passe dat Ich want in pax onder der sonne
sleepe ohne paparazzos around. Recepido?

Euro: Lets aan largo sea mit meine pedalero
navigare und die birds op der sky, die
barquettas op der sea poeticamente regarde

teine hande in meine hande keepingante!

Eura: Patetische und mucho banale avance!
Attempte mit anders!

Euro: Lets aan largo sea mit meine pedalero
navigare, onder nos floridos slips nos hands
infilantes und muchos   kissos op der neck
exchangeantes!

Eura: (jumpante) Vamos!

Euro by largo sea roamingante, eine romantica canzon languido cantante:

Euro: (mit de "Oh sole mio" tune)
Floridos slips strip off aan moi! Floridos
slips strip off aan toi! Floridos die slips wir
stripp und dann wat happen wir know toch
nicht!

Eine sudden hurlo in der aire resounded:

Olde dame: Helpo! Helpo! Ich esse suffocante!

Eine olde dame was in die waves van horrore screamingante.
Euro pronto plonged und atletico op der playa de olde dame
tracted.

Olde dame: Meine heroe! You habe meine life salvaged!
Kissa moi meine amor, kissa moi mucho!

De olde dame embrassed Euro intra seine arms serrante und

passionately over de sand rollante terwhile dat Eura op der pedalero solitaria bronzed seine derriero indifferente.

III

Convesazio curso por europanticos touristos: Zum restorante

Eura esse eine waiteresse in eine renommed Azurrecoast balneare stazion restorante. Euro esse eine raffinado turisto in diese restorante masticante.

Menu:

Spaghetti thonno
Spaghetti crabe
Spaghetti mayonneza
Spaghetti bolognaise

Eura: Gutte eveningo! Wat commande?

Euro: Mmmh! Ich shal Spaghetti thonno commande

Eura: Perdonne meine herr, but van thonno habe nicht plus left!

Euro: Ah! Wat Shame! Dann ich shal Spaghetti crabe commande.

Eura: Perdonne muchissimo meine herr but van crabe habe nicht plus left!

Euro: Ah! Wat double shame! Dann ich shal Spaghetti mayonneza.

Eura: Desolatissimo perdono implorante, monherr, but van mayonneza habe nicht plus left!

Euro: Ah! Wat triple shame! (bit disappointado) Dann hope ich you habe ten minder Spaghetti bolognaise!

Eura: Securamente meine herr! Spaghetti bolognaise esse unsere spezialitas!

De waiteresse make eine reverenza und sich retire gentilmente. Come zuback eine poquito later mit eine dish plain spaghetti. Euro regarde perplexo in der dish und observe:

Euro: Aber dat esse plain spaghetti und basta! Waar esse de bolognaise?

Eura: Moi voilà, meine herr! Ich esse trulymente eine out Bologna spezialitas! Eine pure bolognaise dame! Gut Appetito!

IV

Convesazio curso por europanticos touristos: In der finlandica sauna

Euro, der trueful und unico veritable europeo, esse op vakanza in Finlandia. Eine dag decide in eine sauna te gehen. Er esse mucho vapor und calor. Euro fatiguante transpire quando de porta open und eine siluetta entre.

Euro thinke: "Ollallà, viva die mixtas saunas! Aquì arrive eine bonita dama mit longos blondos capellos! Maintenow ella aborde und tenfinally Ich shal de famoso nordico sex-appeal savourate!"

Euro: Milionissimas excusas, can Ich helpe de towel zum bank distende?

Siluetta: De towel ich shitte op!

Euro thinke: Ah, die nordicas feminas mucho emancipatas esse und make sichzelf keine complexo inderfact! Esse gut! Wir esse in eine democratische societate waar alles esse equales, hombres und damas!

Euro: Ah! Muchissimamante embarassado de disturb. Ich wanted only helpe! Can Ich maybe de glas polish, so dat you shal de beautiful lake mit arcadica foresta contemplate?

Siluetta: Arcadica foresta ich shitte op!

Euro: Ah! Certamently nicht alles people like die lakes. De lake esse dirty, ful van fange, van mosquitos, van bourdones, van crapones. Beter in eine piscina sich plonge! Mademoiselle, like maybe die swimming piscina more?

Siluetta: Swimming piscinas ich shitte op!

Euro thinke: Ah! Diese nordicas feminas habe echte forte caractero! Esse gut! Ich like resolutas personas die know wat want!

Euro: Ah! Esse correcto! In de piscinas shitte esse gut for de gesantheid, purifica und deterge der intestinale interior, so dat man feel beter und plus equilibred esse in seine everydagselife.

Siluetta: Ich shitte op teine everydagse life!

Euro: Eh! Basta esse basta! Mademoiselle, Ich unterstande dat you eine emancipata dama esse, aber can accepte nicht vulgaritates!

Siluetta: Ich shitte op de emancipata dama tambien!
Ich   esse keine emancipata dama!

De siluetta turned sichzelf und let der towel gefallen op soil, aan Euro demonstrante dat in Finlandia never saunas mixtas esse.

V

Conversatio curso por europantouristos: How eine
stradale amenda abstutemente avoide

Euro habe op forbiddo parkingo seine auto geparqued. Van de
sea playa zubackante, finde eine policeresse eine amenda op
seine auto paravento glissante.

Euro: Prosternato und excusante, meine fascinante
soldatesse! Ich departe subito aweg! Perdona
mich! Ich wanted nicht mit meine bad parkingo
toi make suffer!

Eura: (de amenda writingante) Ich suffer nicht por
bad parkingos und amendas make Ich wel
allegramente!

Euro: Aan teine piedones glissante und mich van
repentimento fustigante, meine heroische
colonel! Ich feel dat you esse mit moi mucho
enraged und dat can Ich sopporte nicht!
Alsyouplease, make moi eine smile oder ich
fainto van dolor!

Eura: (toch de amenda writingante) Ich make keine
smile aan unfamiliare people und inutilissimo
esse todas die historias te make por eine

amende!

Euro: Teine masculissimos bootones polissante, meine gaillarda generalesse! Reprimande moi nicht! Ich feel eine pesantissimo complexo van culpa moi suffoquante der corazon!

(Euro falle op soil cryingante. Eura stoppe de write und regarde Euro eine poquito worried)

Eura: Que make? Esse brainsick in der cervelle?

Euro: Meine Presidentesse des Rebubliqua, meine Reine des Kingdom! If you make moi eine amenda, ich shal self suicidio performe, de breath retainingante eine hora durante! Ich shal por toi morto esse in diese foreigno pais, porqué can live nicht if you esse mit moi enraged

(Euro start de breath retain. Eura dann ello embrassed mucho moved)

Eura: Nomanno never dixit moi so sweetissima parolas! Nomanno never offered moi seine llife! Meine amor, kissa me!

Morale des fabula: Tambien dei policeresse habe eine corazon

VI

Conversatio curso por europantouristos: In eine veneziano souveniro marketto

Euro, der trueful europeo, esse in Venezia mit seine maisteresse op vakanza und eine morgen gehe zum lokale marketto por souveniros verfauffe.

Euro: Salve Regina! Habe you eine glass boule mit Eiffeltorre unter snow?

Vendor: Esse stupidose brainsick? Aquì in Venezia esse, keine Paris! Wir habe glass boules mit San Marco unter snow, but keine Eiffeltorre!

Euro: Ah! Dat esse por moi eine probleme, porqué Ich dixit meine wife dat por business in Paris Ich hadde to gehen. Und per contre Ich esse in Venezia mit meine maisteresse traveled!

Vendor: Ah, ah! Ich unterstundo well! Tu esse in der merdenshit zum neck!

Euro: Wat suggeste moi?

Vendor: You can eine San Marco glass boule verkauffe, de San Marco out des boule take und eine Eiffeltorre inside put!

Diego Marani

Euro: Dat esse eine gutte idea, aber where finde ich
          aquì eine Eiffeltorre?

Euro: Ah! Verblodde! Dat hadde Ich thinked nicht!
          Dann habe Ich eine andere idea. You kauffe
          de San Marco glass boule und aan teine wife
          dixit dat esse der novel teatro Olympia van
          Paris!

Euro: Wonderfulle idea! You esse eine genius!
          Bedankes very mucho!

Wir know nicht wat Euro wife dixit de San Marco basilica unter
snow voyante. Aber wir know por sure dat in front van teatro
Olympia in Paris passe gondolas nicht.

Morale des fabula: Siempre de gondolas out des boule take
quando offer teine wife eine glass boule mit San Marco basilica
unter snow.

VII

Conversatio curso por europantouristos: By der mecanico

Op vakanza in Greeklandia, Eura habe seine auto kaput und ella finde eine mucho speziale garage.

Eura: Herr mecanico, der motor van meine auto werke plus nicht. Can moi helpe alsyouplease?

Euro: Keine worry madama! Ich esse der beste, der unique psycomecanico van toda Greeklandia!

Euro open der coffro, permane eine moment auscultante, dann sommige parolas aan der spinterogeno whisper.

Euro: Ah! Ich understuddo. Ah! Triste situatione! Ich pity toi mucho!

Euro dann adresse aan Eura:

Euro: Madama, teine auto habe eine harde depressie porqué ella esse in amore gefallen mit eine autocarro turbo intercooler. Aber ello esse already mit eine autobussa married und habe zwei childrenos, eine moto und eine Vespa.

Eura: Und wat can ich solve diese problema?

Euro: Er esse nada te make. Man must attende dat passe! Take eine hotel stanza und spende some vacante tempo aquì.

Eura: (muchissimo perplexa) Ah! Bedankes mucho. Zum proximo!

Euro: Eine moment madama! Ehm! You habe meine honorario bezaled nicht!

Eura: Ah! Quanto mucho esse?

Euro: Esse zwei thousand euros...

Eura: Wat! Dat esse maxime exagerato expensivo por eine mecanico!

Euro: Liebissime madama, Ich esse keine normale mecanico. Ich esse eine psycomecanico!

Morale des fabula: Autos can sentimentos habe, mecanicos no.

Der Wunderbare Mundo Des Europantide

1 Der wunderbare mundo des Europantide

Diese sommer der Europanto Instituto van Bricopolitik bring toi in Europantide, der wunderbare paterland van europanto, por eine culturale vacatione mit linguistische proficiente course und interessante explorationes van culturale wel leisurale platz. Europantide esse eine feliciose islanda in der middle des Linguistische Ocean. Habe eine mild climate, mit soleadas plages und turqouise maritime wasser, aber op die montagnas man can skifahren todo el jahro. Europantopol, seine citycapital, surge op der maritime side, next des estuario des Mistake river, qui descende des nevose pics van der spectaculaire Mont Plusquamperfect. Der most remarquable monument van Europantopol esse der Babel Turm, eine gigantische constructione gebuilded zum celebrate humane reciproque comprehensione wel tolerance, mit eine panoramische restaurante. Als jedere capitale, Europantopol habe importante museum, zoologicale gardens und pleasante parcs. Seine maritime plage van Quiproquo esse jedere tag full van Europantopolenos, und aquì die Europantopolenos habe seine appointements, make seine business, encounter seine lovers, spiele mit seine bambinos, sunbronze, slape oder savourate eine glas van Irregular, der nationale Europantide drink: eine weisse sweete petillante vino. Next des plage esse der most populaire café van Europantopol: der Lapsus Bar. Aquì reunite die artistische wel intellectuale personalitas des capital, aber tambien studentes und jonge people. Jedere eveningo play eine musicale group. Europantopolenos speak solo europanto, aber unterstande facilemente franzoso, germano, italiano, espanolo, portugueso, finnico, olde greco und latino. Ellos unterstande tambien perfectamente englando, aber adhore de make semblante de lo unterstande nicht. Das esse eine nationale caprice. Als jedere capitale, Europantopol tambien habe seine modes und seine jealousies. Zum exemplo, inhabitantes der rive gauche pretende de esse most intelligente dann die ones des rive droite. Almost todos die Europantides habite Europantopol und Europantopolenos consider eine poquito stupides die inhabitantes op der campagne livingantes. Aber diese esse eine olde historia mit capitales que tambien in der wunderbare mundo van Europantide esse impossible de avoid.

Diego Marani

2 Zum der Centrale Stazion

Der Centrale Stazion van Europantopol esse eine fascinante meeting platz donde siempre interessante cosas happen. Diese stazion esse solo por arrive, nicht por departe. Inderfacts, als departe esse tambien eine poquito sterve, in Europantopol esse departures abolished, por avoid que people inadvertemente sterve und make tristesse cumulate over der stad. So, in der Centrale Stazion tu can solo arrive. Oder tu can gehe zum performe der maxime sophisticated Europantopol sport van train-missing. Train-missing esse por Europantopolenos eine echte art van life que necessite jahros van patiente training por elegante performance. Es handelt inderfacts van miss eine train, aber nicht mit banale gestures. Necessite style und participative implicatione. Dieses qui practice der train-missing sport esse genamed "corridores" und habe in Europantopol eine exclusive reputatione. Aber por miss eine train, eine corrridore no can arrive in der stazion op indifferente tempo. El must exacte calculate der train passage und enter in der stazion op el perfecte momento quando der train passe, quando esse tropo late por lo catch aber nicht tropo late por lo pursue, runningante op el quai mit eine prominente hand versus der portiera des train. Dann, quando der train exit des stazion und der corridore stoppe haletante op el einde des quai, dann el habe seine train elegantemente, participativemente missed. Habitualmente, Europantopolenos regruppe op Centrale Stazion por assiste aan train-missing corridores und applaude beste performance. Der most difficultose challenge por eine corridore esse de miss retardante trains. Porqué por miss punctuale trains esse

127

facile: basta de calculate mit precisione, dann esse solo eine question van elegance. Aber, ter contra, retardante trein esse eine risiko, porqué never know quando exactemente arrive und eine corridore no can absolute disbarque op el quai in advance. Jedere sommer, in Europantopol, op el quinqodeca van augusto eine tournoy esse organized mit beste corridores des island challengeantes eachaltro op diese noble wel profundemente philosophische discipline.

Diego Marani

3 Europantopol linguistische zoo

In der Europantopol zoologicale gardens er esse keine animales, aber toch exemplares van hombres speakante normale europese linguas. Op diese maniera der europantesque civilisatione want preserve aan future generationes eine levende exemplo van antique babelische confusione. So in der Europantopol zoo tu can finde cages mit levende linguistische exemplares van franzosos, germanos, italianos, britannicos, hispanicos, belgicos, swissos. Echtemente, nicht alles cages esse equal : jederuna habe seine ethnische caracteristique. Franzosos stay in eine miniature Paris und before de speak siempre check op el dictionary jedere parole. Van Belgicos esse zwei couples : eine flamingo und die andere wallone. Ellos siempre speak eachaltro mit subtitles. Van swissos er esse dix-und-negen : zwei por jedere romancho, zwei francofonos, zwei alemanofonos und tres ticinofonos, porqué ticinos conserve tambien der grossemutter. Ellos live in eine montagnose garden cage, jederuno op eine differente montagne. Van italianos esse eine couple plus seine respective mammas und muchissimes assiettes und andere dishes por best matrimoniale quarrels. Ellos live in eine grosse kitchen mit televisive apparat siempre on. Van germanos esse eine couple por Land. Ellos speak eachaltro solo in federale hours. Anders, sich regarde ohne speak terwhile preparante jederuno seine differente würst und sippingante der same bier mit differentes names op der bottle. Van britannicos er esse tres couples (scotlandos, gallos und englandos). Spend seine time playingante eine aeternale cricket match donde nomanno know nicht plus not only qui win und qui loose, aber tambien welches squadras spiel. Ellos

129

alles drink tea und speak english solo aan foreigneros, porqué in seine cage speak locale dialectes. In der Europantopol linguistische zoo esse maxime verboten de nourish italianos mit würst oder germanos mit pizzas. Englandos manducate solo BSE beef und chocolate ohne cacao. Belgicos manducate exclusivemente dioxine chicken. As por swissos, por decide wat manducate, ellos siempre necessite de make eine referendum.

Diego Marani

4 Der Metropolitanse Museum van Schone Parolas

Als jedere grande capitale, Europantopol tambien habe
seine artistische institutiones, so als museums und galerias.
Aber Europantopolenos, plus que picturas und sculpturas,
appreciate superalles schone parolas. So in der Europantopol
Metropolitanse Museum van Schone Parolas tu can admire
die most fascinante, elegante, shoquante, mysteriose,
enchantingante, musicale parolas des mundo. Parolas tu can
nicht only admire, aber tambien ausculte, mit compassionate
prononciatione by experte lectores, oder tu can tambien toiself
declamate in speciale interactive microphones. Jedere zwei
jahros take platz in Europantopol der Biennale Expositione,
donde artistes van der whole Europantide come zum presente
seine creative parolas. Die most suggestive ones esse
accepted por expositione. Aber parolas, por esse accepted in
der prestigiose salles des Metropolitanse Museum, necessite
absolute de habe keine significatione. Es must handel van pure
parolas, essentiale sound, ohne reference zum realitate. In case
der jury discover que eine parola admitted in der Museum
habe eine significatione in alcunas linguas des mundo, ella
esse immediate expulsed. Tambien silence esse considered
als creative piece of art und preserved in der Metropolitanse
Museum van Schone Parolas. Porqué nicht alles kind van
silence esse empty und banal. Er existe maxime poetische
silences, allegro, andante silences, tambien tragische oder
mysticale ones. Europantide artistes travel der wholle mundo
op search van suggestive silences und schone parolas ohne

131

significatione zum collecte. Ellas become siempre plus rare zum find, porqué die mucho scarce poetische personas van moderne mundo siempre pretende que jedere parola habe eine precise significatione, que alles must esse unterstandible und expliquable. As por silences, ellos existe quasi plus. Und ohne silence, alles humane parolas, charged mit tropo much significationes, todag suffoquate in eine magma van undistincte noise. Voilà porqué der Metropolitanse Museum van Europantopol collecte rare parolas und silences: por preserve in der tempo diese most preciose product des humane mind.

5 Sexuale und amorose habitos des Europantopolenos

In Europantide, amorose relationes esse mucho festose und spontaneose. Nicht only humanos, aber tambien animalos op terra, birds op sky und pisces op mare, in der season des amor, warmosemente communicate eachaltro seine affectione und libremente exchange sentimentale effusiones. Europantopolenos esse maxime romantische personas und fidelmente respecte der antiqua traditione de proclame seine amor mit poetische serenades unter des balcony van seine beloved. Dat esse porqué jedere haus van Europantopol hav´be seine balcony, tambien die most modeste ones. So, superalles in tepide springtempose nacht, tu can ausculte in der stradas van Europantopol sweetose canzones und languide refrainellos van amorose pretendentes navigate in der aire. Jedere jahro in majo take platz in der Municipale Theatre van Europantopol der Nationale Serenade Festival, donde die beste serenades receive eine prize und esse recorded op disco por become der musicale tubes des europantopolense sommer que jederuno danse in populaire fiestas op der playa. Voilà der text van diese jahro winningante serenade

"Amor wat make":

Amor wat make behind die fenestre?
Entende nicht diese tempeste
Que ohne rain und ohne föhn
Make explodente mein corazön?
Amor approache van die balcone

smell quanto forte mein love perfume
que make vanish van de springtempo
alles die flowers op ein momento!

In Europantide, Viagra bestaat nicht: er esse keine necessitas.
Porqué esse bastante der refrain van eine serenade por make
surge alles wat must surge in amorose affaires. Inderfacts,
in Europantide amorose affectione esse held in maxima
consideratione und esse protected mit soziale securitas.
Quando alcuno fall innamorated, el habe der right van eine
ohne solde "amorose leave", por sich consacrate full tempo
aan seine passion und returne zum werk solo quando habe
sichself totaal disfouled, oder quando seine amor evaporated
mit der amorose season.

6 Europantide nationale fiesta

Der tag des nationale fiesta in Europantide esse der primero van april. Op diese memorable date, manige manifestationes celebrate der founding des Libera Linguistische Republica des Europantide. Op el morning, eine parade van vocabularios in alles linguas des mundo traverse der Europantopol city centre und range op der maritime promenade, donde Europantopolenos can visit und consulte diese rare operas. Dann der Presidente des Republica gehe depose eine gerbe van flowers op der monument aan des Unbekannte Mistake, qui esse der sacred heroe des Europanto ideale. Porqué inderfacts, esse der mistake qui keep jedere lingua alive und la make progress towards der future. Ohne mistakes, linguas woudde slowemente disappear, porqué unable de sich adapte aan der changingante welt. In der history des linguas, jedere mistake presto oder later become correcte und wat esse mistake todag esse rule tomorrow. Europantide becomed eine independente linguistische respublica mit der liberatione guerra des 1848, quando die Europantopolenos pouchassed der tirannische regime van der Grammaticale Inquisitione mit der famous Verbale Revolutione. In der tempo des Grammaticale Inquisitione, grammaticale rigor was maxime severe. Secreta polizia coudde improvisto arreste people op strada und pregunte op surpirse grammaticale rules. Jedere grammaticale mistake oder lapsus was punished mit prison und eine verfehled subjonctive coudde coste aan Europantopolenos der mortale punishment. Exhausted por eine so repressive regime, op der morning des 1 avrilo 1848, die Europantopolenos launched eine revolutione. Ellos marched alles ensemble in die stradas van Europantopol, forte shoutingante alles die mistakes van alles die linguas des mundo. Grammarius XXXIV, der ultime rex des Grammaticale Inquisitione, coudde nicht supporte eine similare schock und infarctuose trespassed al creator. Por celebrate der liberatione, op el platz van seine grammaticale palace, die Europantopolenos builded der moderne Babel Turm, qui mit seine multilinguale diversitas celebrate der liberatione des lingua van alles rules.

Diego Marani

7 Europantide colossale trafic marmelade

So als jedere grande citystadt, tambien Europantide suffer
from endemicale trafic problemas. Superalles op el morning
zum nine horas und op el postmeridio zum quinquo horas, alles
die peripherale boulevardes esse saturated mit commutante
werkers nach der büro oder zuruck zum casa travellantes.
Aber tambien in traficale inferno, Europantopolenos maintain
seine elegante style van life und never claxonne. Inderfacts,
claxones op Europantide autowagen werke nicht. Ter platz van
claxones, jedere autowagen habe eine microphone donde der
conductor can expresse seine sentimentos oder seine critiques
zum communicate aloud aan die andere conductores por
eine proficiente traficale dialectique. Tambien insultes esse
admitted, mit der contition que esse sophisticated und acute.
Quando eine insulte esse brutale, jedere conductore whistle
seine disappointement und der plate number des conductore
qui pronounced die inconveniente parolas esse recorded by
eine polizero por eine lessicale amende oder eine temporaire
microphone sequestratione. So, nomanno shal never dixit
"Cretinus" oder "Imbecillis" aan eine conductor schlechte
behaviorante op eine crossestrada, aber most elegante
sentencias, zoals: "Donde was quando intelligenzia was
distributed?" oder "Porqué insiste in kauffe wasmaschine ter
platz van echte autowagen?" oder "Stop de schumacherate!"
oder "Habe eine drivingante licence oder eine fishingante one?",
oder "Phanales op autowagen esse nicht als licht in flipper:
tu win niks quando smashe one!". Die beste traficale insultes
esse published in reclame pancartas along des autostrada, zum
teaching por negligente conductores. Europantide habe toch

137

eine mucho efficiente metropolitain, aber nicht bastante por solve traficale emergencias. Metropolitain lines esse quatro und habe maxime poeticale names: Presens (rosso color), Past (blaue color) und Future (yellow color). Most importantes Europantide metropolitain stationes habe der name van: Exception, Equivoque, Verba volant. Der ticket esse gratis: por bezale must solo dixit eine pleasante complimento aan der ticketteuse.